My life behind the scenes at...

Heart
Magazine

My life behind the scenes at...

Heart Magazine

A dream come true

Cindy Jefferies

USBORNE

For Megan and Anne, two editors to *die* for

First published in 2011 by Usborne Publishing Ltd., Usborne House,
83-85 Saffron Hill, London EC1N 8RT, England.
www.usborne.com

JFM MJJASOND/11 02345/1 ISBN 9781409520207
Printed in Reading, Berkshire, UK.

1
A glamorous job

"You can hang your coat through here." The girl with the perfectly groomed, long blonde hair held the door open for Ellie, swaying slightly on her vertiginously high heels. Her mouth smiled, but she wasn't actually looking at Ellie, and her highly glossed lips seemed more designed for pouting than for smiling. In fact the smile faded almost instantly, and was replaced by a look of irritation that made it obvious how much of a nuisance Ellie was, just by being there.

But Ellie Ixos wasn't going to allow herself to be intimidated. She might only be here at the Editorial Department at *Heart* magazine for two weeks' work experience, but for her it was a huge deal to have got this placement. For a start, she'd had to overcome her mum's doubts about even considering it.

"If you're interested in fashion, why not approach one of the shops?" her mum had said. "A couple of weeks selling clothes would be fun, and you'd probably get a discount on anything you wanted to buy."

Ellie felt cross. She knew that Mum *hated* the idea of Ellie becoming a journalist, as her father had been. "But I don't want to *sell* clothes," she'd said. "I want to *write* about them – and other things too." She saw the expression on her mum's face and struggled to be diplomatic. "It's not *dangerous*," she said. "*Heart* is a teen magazine! I've even looked up the bus times. I only have to catch two. Hannah has to get the train and walk loads to get to the city farm where she's working. I'll be fine. Honestly. Besides" – Ellie tried to sound apologetic, but her voice was firm – "everyone in the class has to file a report about their work experience, and the best will go up on the school website. *I* want to be up there, where the action is."

A shadow passed across Georgia Ixos's face, and Ellie wished she hadn't mentioned being where the action was.

Then her mum's expression softened and she sighed. "You've got your dad's determination. I'm sure he'd have said to go ahead, so I shouldn't try to stop you, should I?"

Ellie gave her mum a hug, which said sorry as well as thank you. "So you'll ask Uncle Patrick?"

Ellie's dad had been a foreign correspondent. He had lost his life reporting from a war zone shortly before Ellie was born, so she could understand why her mum was wary of her daughter wanting to become a journalist too.

But Uncle Patrick was her dad's older brother, and he was on the board of *Heart*. The magazine was Ellie's favourite, and exactly the sort she dreamed of working for.

Mum hugged her back. "*You* ask Uncle Patrick. You can't be a journalist if you're scared of asking favours!"

It *had* been a bit scary, phoning Uncle Patrick. Ellie couldn't remember ever meeting him. Apparently, although he'd been very helpful with money when her dad had been killed, Uncle Patrick had been angry at his brother's death and seemed to blame everyone, including Georgia, for what happened. Georgia felt he had been totally unreasonable. As a result they'd fallen out and hadn't met for years.

"As if I could have stopped your dad," Georgia told Ellie one day when she was reminiscing about the past. "Even with me being pregnant he still had to go. He had a burning desire to tell the truth about bad situations. He said he owed it to all the people being killed out there." Georgia sighed and put her arm round her daughter. "He'd have loved you so much," she said sadly. "I do wish he'd been able to see you, at least once, but your father was just as stubborn as you are sometimes. Anyway," she added briskly, "no point dwelling on it now. It was a long time ago."

Ellie knew that she had a stubborn streak, and it was rather nice to feel she had something in her of the dad she'd never met. Maybe her interest in writing was inherited from him too? There was no danger, though, that Ellie would follow him into a war zone. Fashion, boy bands and animal welfare were more her kind of thing at the moment. She had *always* wanted to be a journalist, and she simply loved the glossy magazines that mixed fashion and celebrity gossip with articles on more important issues. Especially *Heart*, because they always seemed to interview the people Ellie liked best.

Actually, speaking to Uncle Patrick had been fine. Ellie had thought up all sorts of reasons to persuade him to let her do her work experience at his magazine, but she hadn't needed any of them.

"Of course you can," he'd said straight away. "I'll let them know when to expect you. Maybe I'll come along and take you out to lunch one day if I can schedule it in." He'd paused, and then Ellie had heard him laugh. "I can't believe you're all grown up. I met you once, but you were a tiny baby."

"Well!" Georgia had said when Ellie told her. "I suppose he did meet you, but he didn't take a lot of interest. I think he was scared of babies, and you were only a few weeks old." She'd given her daughter a smile. "Maybe he's ready to be friends now."

But all that had happened weeks ago. Since

then, Ellie had been waiting impatiently for her first day at the magazine to arrive. Now, at last, it had and she couldn't help feeling rather intimidated. It would have been different if she'd known Uncle Patrick well – he might have offered to meet her and show her round – but she was on her own as she got off the bus and approached the place where she was going to work for the next two weeks.

Ellie was bright, strong-willed and confident, but she was undeniably awed by the huge, steel-and-glass office building that housed *Heart, Soul – Heart*'s sister magazine – and a dozen other magazines that were owned by the same company. She needed to take a deep breath to steady her nerves before approaching the reception desk in the main lobby. After that, waiting for someone to come down from *Heart* and take her up to the editorial office was just as nerve-wracking. The busy lobby seemed full of glamorous people, and when a tall, beautiful, blonde girl arrived to guide her to the lifts, Ellie's heart quivered.

"Hi," said the girl, neglecting to tell Ellie her name. "You're the work experience girl, aren't you?" The expression on the blonde girl's face made it clear that she didn't feel enthusiastic about having to look after a student. But in the lift, while the girl rudely ignored her, Ellie had time to gather herself. She was determined to enjoy her placement, so by the time they left the lift she had told herself she was feeling in control and not a bit scared.

Even so, here she was, fumbling with a mixture of nerves and excitement to put her very ordinary coat on the swanky, velvet-covered hanger that had been handed to her. The hanger was emblazoned with the name of a major fashion designer, and somehow it made her coat look decidedly shabby. The blonde girl rolled her eyes skywards. Ellie's coat was dangling crookedly, and the girl's expression made it clear that such slovenliness was not going to be acceptable. Ellie hurriedly adjusted her coat to make it look neater. The other coats and jackets on the rail managed to look intimidating, just by hanging there so perfectly, and the bored expression on the girl's beautifully made-up face didn't help, but Ellie refused to feel daunted. She was here, and it was still a dream come true!

Ellie had taken loads of care with her clothes and make-up. She had discussed it endlessly with Hannah, her best friend at school, and hoped she'd got it about right.

"You want to look good, but you also want to be taken seriously as a wannabe journalist, don't you?" Hannah had said.

So, rather than a minidress, she'd chosen her favourite top and trousers and her cool, new boots that she utterly loved. She reckoned she'd got her look just about right...fashionable, but professional too. Her mum didn't let her wear too much make-up anyway, but today they were in agreement. There was no point in Ellie trying to look twenty, when the staff would all know she was fourteen and still at school. Even so, as soon as she'd left the house, Ellie put another layer of mascara on, just to be sure.

Naturally, she'd got this month's copy of *Heart* in her bag, and something her mum had given her just before she'd left to catch the bus.

"Here you are." Georgia had thrust an old-fashioned-looking black notebook into her daughter's hands. "It was your father's. He bought it before his last trip and then forgot to take it with him."

"Thanks, Mum." Ellie had been touched, but the notebook wasn't exactly the sort of thing she expected journalists at *Heart* would use. She was thrilled to have something of her dad's, but it was so old-fashioned it would be embarrassing if anyone at *Heart* saw it. Ellie had stuffed it into her bag, and run down the road just in time to catch the bus.

Now she hurried again, so as not to keep the blonde girl waiting. She followed her through the lobby and towards the office. Ellie had just caught a tantalizing glimpse of workstations, expensive-looking chairs and an expanse of white carpet when the girl came to such a sudden halt that Ellie almost bumped into her.

"Didn't they tell you to bring a pair of office shoes?"

Ellie looked down at her feet. For a moment she had no idea what the girl meant: then a sudden image entered her head. It was of herself, walking along that white carpet in her new boots, dark from the rain and grubby from the pavement. She would leave marks everywhere! She found herself blushing with embarrassment. "Uncle Patrick didn't say anything about shoes," she said, annoyed with herself for sounding so pathetic.

The girl tossed her long blonde hair in annoyance and muttered "Honestly!" just loud enough for Ellie to hear. "Come on then." She pushed past Ellie with a sigh and went back into the lobby. For an awful moment Ellie thought she was going to be thrown out, but the girl was opening a cupboard to reveal a jumbled collection of high-heeled shoes. "What size are you?"

"Five." Ellie was determined not to let this setback get to her.

The girl waved dismissively at the shoes and turned to go. "Once you've found something that fits, put your boots *neatly* in the other cupboard and come into the office. I don't have time to wait."

Ellie crouched down and looked at the shoes in despair. She had never found walking in heels particularly easy, and all these shoes had heels way higher than anything she was used to. For an instant she wondered if she could get away with bare feet, but she knew in her bones that no *way* would that be acceptable in the *Heart* office.

She discarded the first pair she looked at straight away. They were covered with beads and feathers, and the heels were so spiky you could toast marshmallows on them. In fact, all the shoes seemed ridiculously over the top for a day at the office. But at the back of the cupboard she found a pair of sandals that looked a bit less difficult to walk in. They were probably the least trendy of the lot, but she loved the soft red leather of the straps and, to her relief, they fitted well enough. They looked pretty cool too.

As soon as she'd stowed her boots in the outdoor shoes cupboard she pulled herself awkwardly to a standing position. She felt about half a metre taller. The soles of the shoes were curved and, as she took her first steps, she found herself rolling towards the office through the thick carpet. It made her feel a little queasy, as if she were on a boat.

At the door she paused for a moment. She wanted to make sure she wasn't in danger of bumping her head on the lintel, but told herself not to be so ridiculous. The shoes hadn't made her *that* tall.

Entering the office by herself was undeniably scary, but she'd got this far, and Ellie was in no way a quitter.

I have every right to be here, she told herself firmly. *And I won't let myself be put off by* anything *or* anybody!

Resisting the impulse to look at her feet as she walked, she held her head high and pushed open the door. The blonde girl was nowhere to be seen, but another very pretty girl, with glossy brown hair, was sitting at a desk by the door. She looked up and smiled at Ellie. "*Heart*, the magazine to die for," she said. "Editorial Department. Can I help you?"

Ellie's heart leaped on hearing the famous words that appeared every month on the front of the magazine. "Yes," she said, trying to keep her voice level in spite of it wanting to bubble over with excitement. "I'm Ellie Ixos. Here on my work experience placement."

For a moment the girl frowned, then her face cleared. "Oh yes. Ellie." She smiled again. "Is Patrick Ixos a relation? It's a very unusual name."

Ellie nodded.

The receptionist looked pleased with herself. "Thought so." She paused. "Isn't Pea-Are-No looking after you?"

"Well...someone met me in the lobby..." Ellie didn't want to admit that the blonde girl hadn't actually introduced herself, and she certainly wasn't going to mention the coat or shoe incidents.

"Honestly! Trust her to desert you!" The girl pushed her chair back and got up. "Okay, I'll do it. I'm Carlotta Spender-Jones." She offered her rather limp hand with its long, dark purple nails, and Ellie shook it, wondering how Carlotta managed the keyboard with such talons. "Don't worry if you forget our names," said Carlotta. "We all have them on our desks, so you can easily sneak a look without having to admit you can't remember." She giggled, and Ellie warmed to her. She looked a bit younger than Pea-Are-No, and although she was obviously a lot older than fourteen, Ellie hoped they might become friends. "Follow me then. I'll give you a quick whisk around the office. This is Pea-Are-No's desk."

Ellie peered at the name on the desk and almost burst out laughing. The way Carlotta had pronounced the name, Ellie had wondered if it was oriental, but it was spelled Piano, like the instrument! Piano Arnley-Armitage. What a ridiculous name. No wonder she didn't like saying it the way it was spelled! But Carlotta had moved on.

"This is Francesca Mosse's desk. She's the Deputy Editor. And this" – Carlotta pointed one beautifully manicured finger – "is Flynn, doing something weird to Francesca's laptop. He's our IT whizz-kid."

To Ellie, Flynn looked more like gorgeous, boy-band material than an IT expert and, judging by Carlotta's fluttering eyelashes, she thought so too. But when he glanced up he showed no sign of appreciating her flirtatious behaviour. He ignored her and grinned at Ellie instead. "Hi!" He reached out his hand and shook hers firmly. "You must be here on work experience. I hope these dragons don't put you off. If you get fed up, go down and see Sophie in the post room. She'll sort you out." Then he flashed Carlotta a cheeky smile and went back to prising the keyboard off the laptop. "By the way," he added casually, prodding the inside of the laptop with a tiny screwdriver as he spoke, "I'm not doing anything weird. There's a little battery in here that needs resetting." He replaced the keyboard and looked very pleased with himself.

Carlotta frowned. "One day you'll break something, fiddling about like that," she said. Then, glancing round the otherwise deserted office, she looked puzzled. "Where is everyone?"

"Francesca and Piano went into the lion's den with Joe."

"Without me?" Carlotta clicked her tongue in annoyance. "Francesca said they'd try to discuss the next shoot when I wasn't busy, so I could be included. Reception work is supposed to be shared, but it's always *me* who has to do it!" She marched through the office, with Ellie trailing behind, wondering what the "lion's den" was – and if Piano minded Flynn pronouncing her name like an instrument.

Carlotta led Ellie through a glass panelled door and into a large, beautifully furnished inner office. On the door, was a sign that said: *Angel Makepiece – Editor in Chief.* That must be the lion's den. Flynn's name for it didn't exactly inspire confidence! Ellie could see several people inside. One overshadowed the rest. She was a stunningly beautiful woman, with glowing dark brown skin over a perfect bone structure. Her black hair was scraped back off her face and her make-up was flawless. She would have been tall even without the heels she wore. Her pale cream shirt and pencil skirt oozed authority, and echoed the faultless beauty of the lilies in the vase beside her.

As Carlotta and Ellie approached, the woman turned her cool brown eyes on them both. Ellie decided to be brave, and grown-up, and introduce herself.

"I'm Ellie," she said, stepping into the office and offering her hand to the sophisticated woman. "I expect my Uncle Patrick told you about me."

A sudden silence fell, and everyone in the room stared at Ellie. The woman's stunning eyes widened slightly, and her mouth twitched into the barest hint of a smile. "He didn't speak to me," she said in a rich voice that seemed to reverberate through the office, although it was actually quite quiet. "I'm afraid you've made a mistake. I'm Francesca Mosse, the Deputy Editor. He probably spoke to Angel, our Editor in Chief."

"Yes," stammered Ellie, withdrawing her hand and feeling about two years old. "Of course." If she hadn't been wearing such ridiculous shoes she could have kicked herself. It was obvious that the woman wasn't the editor. She looked nothing like the photograph that appeared inside the front cover of the magazine every month. But how could Ellie explain that she hadn't noticed the real editor, because she'd been totally overshadowed in her own office by her deputy? It would hardly be diplomatic!

Ellie looked at Angel Makepiece, who was standing next to a huge, impressive desk. The photograph in the magazine made her seem friendly as well as glamorous. She didn't look friendly at the moment, but she certainly was glamorous. Her clothes were sophisticated and obviously expensive, but her expression was icy. Was that because Ellie had ignored her in her own office? Why should Angel Makepiece seem so angry over a simple mistake made by a work experience girl? Then Ellie remembered Uncle Patrick. He was on the board of the magazine. Had he foisted Ellie on Angel against her wishes? Maybe Uncle Patrick hadn't done her such a big a favour after all.

Ellie's heart dropped to the soles of her red

25

office sandals. The last thing she needed was to be resented by the editor just for being here, but she'd hardly done herself any favours either. Ellie had so wanted to make a good impression, but with the shoe incident and now this, all she'd done so far was to make a fool of herself. Had she made an enemy too?

2
A friend in need

Ellie tried to make the best of a difficult situation by smiling tentatively at the Editor. Angel Makepiece was an attractive woman, with short, artfully styled, blonde hair and a soft round face with a pink and white complexion. She was wearing a beautifully cut, dove-grey dress, and an expression that didn't soften in the slightest at Ellie's smile. In fact, she looked right through Ellie without even acknowledging her.

"How dare you leave your desk," she told Carlotta in a steely voice, still ignoring Ellie completely. "You're on reception duty. Piano, give the student something to do. And keep it out of the way."

Ellie felt outraged at being referred to as "it", but at that moment she was far too crushed to object. She was distracted by a hairy, ethnic-looking handbag, which the Editor was clutching under her arm. Ellie didn't mean to stare so hard, but the bag looked totally incongruous in these glossy surroundings. Then, to her astonishment, the handbag gave a wriggle and a tiny, black pointed nose appeared. Two little brown eyes looked at Ellie. And from behind Angel's arm, a long hairy tail began to wag. In spite of her discomfort, Ellie had an almost overwhelming desire to giggle.

"Coffee, Piano," the Editor continued, playing with the dog's ears and totally ignoring both Ellie and Carlotta. "And bring one for Francesca and Joe too. We have to get this shoot decided."

Ellie wrenched her gaze away from the dog. Carlotta had already scuttled back to the reception desk, and so Ellie looked to Piano to tell her what to do. But the girl who had brought her up in the lift was looking almost as angry as Angel. It seemed to Ellie as though some people in *Heart*'s editorial office wasted a lot of energy being furious, and that most of their fury was currently directed at her. Then she noticed a dark-haired, middle-aged man wearing glasses and a crumpled linen jacket, leaning against the Editor's desk. He must be Joe. He was offering her a sympathetic smile, but before she could respond, Piano took her elbow in a painful grip and steered her out of the office. She closed the door behind them before releasing Ellie.

"You. Follow me," said Piano, in a cold voice.

"Okay," agreed Ellie, rubbing her elbow. She felt totally snubbed and deflated, but she wasn't going to let Piano, or Pea-Are-No, (however she preferred her ridiculous name to be pronounced) see that. After all, it wasn't Ellie's fault Piano had been told to look after her.

Piano gathered up some papers on her way past Francesca's desk and tottered on to her own desk, trailing Ellie behind like the tail of a kite. Flynn raised his eyebrows to Ellie as she scuttled past and she gave him as big a smile as she could manage, which wasn't much of one.

Piano sat down at her desk and pulled a stack of envelopes towards her. "Put the letters into these envelopes, making sure you match the name on the letter with the right envelope." Her tone of voice made Ellie feel like a three year old. Piano held the stationery out to Ellie without looking at her. "I assume you are capable of doing that?"

Ellie took the bundle, feeling very hard done by. "Of course I can. You just fold them up and..."

Piano sighed. "You'd better show me. Go on. Do the first one here."

Ellie felt more like poking Piano in the eye than demonstrating her envelope-stuffing skills, but she gritted her teeth and tried to keep her voice level. "Okay." She looked at the name on the first envelope and matched it to a letter addressed to the same person. It wasn't difficult, as the envelopes and letters had obviously been produced in order. "Right?" she enquired, showing Piano that the names matched. Piano nodded with a long-suffering expression on her face. Ellie folded the letter in half and was just about to fold it again when Piano squealed. Ellie almost dropped the letter.

"Not like that!"

"What do you mean?"

Piano snatched the letter out of Ellie's hand, muttering under her breath. "You don't just fold it any old how. It's A4 paper. You fold the letter in three like this. See? Don't you learn anything at school?"

Deftly, Piano folded the sheet equally into three, and slid it into the envelope. It fitted perfectly. She sealed the envelope and tapped it with her dark nails, then looked at Ellie and sighed again, extravagantly this time. She took a few sheets of plain paper and added them to the pile of letters and envelopes. "Go away and practise. When you've got it right, come back and show me, before you mangle any more letters. Okay?"

Ellie took the heap, feeling totally humiliated. "Where shall I go?" she asked meekly.

Piano pointed to the reception desk, where Carlotta was sitting. "Take that spare chair and go over there," she said. "The reception desk is big enough for two."

Carlotta seemed just as friendly as she had done to begin with. "Don't worry about Piano," she said. "Since she was promoted to Angel's Personal Assistant she's been impossible. But she's no better than you or me." Carlotta eyed the pile of stationery and smiled. "Forget the plain paper," she advised. "You have to divide plain paper into thirds just by eye, but letters are much easier. Look. Estimate which line of writing is a third of the way up, and which is two thirds and make your folds there. Then you'll get it right every time."

"Thanks," said Ellie gratefully. "But Pia…she, said I had to show her a properly folded piece of plain paper before I could do the letters."

Carlotta rolled her eyes. "Here." She folded a plain sheet almost without looking at it and passed it to Ellie. "Take that over to her in a few minutes."

Ellie looked at the folded sheet admiringly. "That's brilliant!" she said. "Thank you so much. Now I can get these letters done straight away." She smiled at Carlotta, hoping she might have found at least one friend in the office.

"Anything you need to know, just ask," said Carlotta.

33

* * *

But in spite of Carlotta's friendliness, by the time Ellie had finished the letters to Piano's approval, and had hung around for ages waiting for Flynn to find her a spare laptop to work on, she was beginning to wonder if she was cut out to work on a glossy magazine. She hadn't come within a whisker of anything journalistic yet. Angel and Francesca were still holed up in Angel's office and, in spite of being sent in twice with coffee for them, they hadn't so much as acknowledged Ellie's presence. Piano had been summoned by Francesca at one point, and was now making numerous phone calls with an exasperated expression on her face. Ellie hadn't a clue what was going on, and no one seemed inclined to explain.

"Don't worry about it," said Carlotta vaguely. "It's always manic here."

"But I'd like to learn a bit about how it all works," said Ellie.

Carlotta sighed. "Okay." She swivelled her chair round so she faced Ellie. "Well. The thing is, most people think that magazines are written one issue at a time, but it doesn't work like that. In the next few days, next month's copy will be going to the printers, so Angel is making last-minute changes and a few finishing touches. But at the same time, she and Francesca are planning what to have in the issue after that, and also" – Carlotta took a deep breath – "things like the bumper Christmas issue need planning *months and months* ahead so that everything gets done in time. Got it?"

"Phew!" Ellie smiled. "It does sound pretty full on. But why make changes so near going to print?"

"Because we need to be as up to the minute as possible, and sometimes things happen just as we're approaching our deadline...like a band splitting up, or a fashion model getting in the news for falling off the catwalk, for instance.

We don't want to have to wait a whole month before writing about it!"

"Yes," Ellie nodded. "I can see that. So some articles have to be written at the last minute. Do you write any of those?"

Carlotta frowned. "I haven't written many full-length articles since I've been here," she admitted. "Mostly it's been just a few small pieces. But it's my turn next. Francesca says I'm nearly ready to have a go at something bigger, and I'm hoping maybe to do a celebrity interview one day. That would be brilliant."

"Wouldn't it!" said Ellie, liking Carlotta more and more.

The reception desk wasn't busy and Ellie was sure that if she had been Carlotta she'd have spent a while practising her article-writing skills, but maybe she'd done that loads of times already. Instead, she spent ages emailing her boyfriend, while Ellie tried not to read the emails over her shoulder. There was still no sign of a laptop, and although she knew she should be patient – because she was the least important person in the building – she almost felt like going home. She had assumed that she would be given articles to write straight away, and would meet loads of famous people. The magazine was always mentioning celebrities who had just dropped into the office. But not today. Carlotta didn't seem to mind being underemployed, but Ellie certainly did. She was so bored she was almost tempted to go and tidy out the shoe cupboard.

At last, Piano put her phone down, with a grumpy face, and noticed Ellie. "Haven't you taken those letters to the post?" she demanded.

"You didn't—" But Piano didn't give her a chance to explain. She picked up her phone again and keyed in yet another number.

Carlotta handed the letters to Ellie with a grin.

"Where's the nearest postbox?" asked Ellie in a whisper, feeling annoyed with Carlotta for neglecting to tell her. "And what about the stamps?"

Carlotta giggled. "You don't leave the building," she said, as if Ellie should have known. "You take them to the post room. Downstairs in the basement."

"And make sure Sophie knows that they must go first class," shouted Piano from the other side of the office, with her ear to the phone. "Without fail."

Ellie took the letters and hurried out.

The post room was most unattractive. The cream, gloss-painted walls were scuffed and worn, and the floor was bare wood. It was very different from the swish *Heart* offices upstairs. There was a large trolley parked near the door, with some post loaded on it. Dividing the room from the corridor was a long, high counter, behind which sat a cheerful-looking girl dressed in a plain jumper and jeans.

"Hi! I'm Sophie," she said. "You must be Ellie."

"Hi," said Ellie, unprepared for Sophie's broad smile, and not really trusting it, even though the girl's clothes and hair looked reassuringly ordinary. "Piano asked me to tell you that these letters have to go first class—"

"Without fail," finished Sophie with a laugh.

"She did say that," agreed Ellie.

"When I deliver mail to the office she often has something to post, and she always says the same thing. Hey, you look as miserable as I'd be if I had to work up there. Fancy a coffee and a biscuit?"

"Well..." Ellie said. "I think I'm supposed to be going straight back up. And I want to see if Flynn has found me a laptop yet."

Sophie looked unconvinced. "You mean they actually *want* you in their witches' coven?"

To her great discomfort, Ellie found herself half laughing and half crying at the same time. She leaned her arms on the counter, put down her bundle of post and buried her head in her arms to try and hide her tears, while she regained her composure.

Sophie took a packet of biscuits out of a drawer and pushed it towards her. "Come round my side and sit down. I'll put the kettle on. I wouldn't hold your breath for a laptop today. There's some horrendous IT problem going on in the Advertising Department at the moment. Flynn is up to his eyes."

In no time they were sitting opposite each other at a plain wooden table, with mugs in their hands and mouths full of chocolate biscuit.

"The nicest person in the office seems to be Flynn," Ellie told Sophie through biscuit crumbs. "He told me to come and see you if I got fed up."

"Did he?" said Sophie, with a pleased

expression on her face, "I think he's great too, but then I would. He's my boyfriend."

"Is he?" Ellie felt a bit awkward. She hoped Sophie wouldn't think she was trying to nab him for herself. Then she blushed. Of course she wouldn't. Flynn was far too old for someone like Ellie. But he was undeniably nice!

"How did you know who I was?" she asked. "I didn't say. I could have come from any of the offices."

Sophie laughed. "That's Flynn for you. He hates to see people being bullied. He texted me to look out for the new work experience girl in the Editorial Department." Then she looked serious. "Why make life hard for yourself?" she said. "Why not go and do your work experience somewhere where you'll actually be appreciated and have fun?"

Ellie took a deep breath and explained about her dad, her mum and Uncle Patrick. "I don't want to give in now Mum has agreed," she explained. "And I'm hoping that Uncle Patrick *will* call in and see me one day. I'd like to get to know him. Besides, I really do want to be a journalist on a magazine, and this is a good start."

"In that case, the first thing you need to do is to know what you're up against," said Sophie. "I can give you the lowdown on all the staff. I get to see and hear a lot while I'm delivering mail, and Flynn does too. They're much easier to cope with once you have the measure of them."

"Brilliant!" said Ellie, beginning to feel a bit better.

"Okay. Now listen: top of the tree is Angel, but she's not your typical, Christmas tree angel. She may look harmless, but she's totally ruthless, very intelligent, and will walk all over you if it suits her. Her only soft spot is for Ferdinand."

"Is that her husband?" asked Ellie.

42

Sophie gave Ellie a playful shove across the table. "No! He's her dog. That ratty little thing she carries everywhere with her. A husband would get in the way of her career, I expect."

"Oh." Ellie began to giggle. "I thought he was a handbag when I first saw him."

Sophie burst into peals of infectious laughter. "I never thought of him like that," she giggled. "He's...Prada with paws!"

"Or...a Gucci growler," suggested Ellie.

When they'd both stopped laughing Sophie carried on. "Francesca is the only one who's married," she said. "Everyone else is on the prowl, but I think they scare off most of the men they meet. Francesca is by far the best and nicest person here."

"Really?" Ellie was surprised. "She's amazing looking, but she scared me rigid. I was so dazzled by her I didn't even notice Angel at first and that didn't go down very well with the Editor in Chief."

"I can imagine," said Sophie, sympathetically. "But Francesca seems very fair. She's got extremely high standards, that's all. You don't need to worry about upsetting her unless you mess up the magazine, which you won't have a chance to do on a couple of weeks' work experience. I'll tell you what though..."

"What?"

"Well" – Sophie settled herself more comfortably – "I got this from Flynn, who listens to all the office gossip. According to him, Angel sees Francesca as a bit of a threat."

"Really?" said Ellie.

"Really. Because before Angel was appointed, Francesca did a very good job of running the magazine, and she's just waiting for Angel to make a mistake and then she'll walk into her job."

"Wow!" said Ellie. Then she paused. "But if she was that good, why didn't she get the job in the first place?"

Sophie grinned. "That's office gossip for you. It doesn't always make sense. But Flynn reckons Angel was appointed because after her degree she worked at a high-profile magazine, whereas Francesca came up the hard way – office junior straight from school – and, well... in-house staff can often get overlooked. Imagine how cool it would be if she did get the top job one day though. Hey!" She nudged Ellie.

"What?"

"I wonder if your uncle is one of the people who helps choose the editors? I bet he is." She smiled comfortably at Ellie. "In which case you don't need to worry about making an enemy of Angel. She'll be on her best behaviour all the time with you."

Ellie shook her head. "I doubt it. If she thinks I have any influence over my uncle she couldn't be more wrong. Anyway, that's Angel and Francesca. Now tell me about Piano."

"Ah." Sophie grinned. "The lovely Pea-Are-No. Do you know, her full name is Elfin Piano Arnley-Armitage, but she dropped the Elfin for being too *Lord of the Rings*. She thinks Piano is more classy, but only Carlotta pronounces it how she prefers and, to be honest, I think even Carlotta is teasing."

"I am finding it hard not to laugh at her name," said Ellie, stifling a giggle.

"She so likes to put on airs and graces," said Sophie. "But really her job is all about keeping Angel's diary up to date, bringing her coffee when she can't get Carlotta to do it and generally keeping her happy. In between writing articles of course, like they all do. Most of the writing is done in the editorial office."

"That leaves Carlotta," said Ellie. "I'm getting on with her really well. She seems nice."

"That's good," said Sophie. "But I bet she likes you because at last there's someone more lowly than a receptionist."

"She's just the receptionist then?" said Ellie. "I thought they shared that role."

"Well I have no idea what her job description is," said Sophie, "but most of the time she seems to be on reception duty. Flynn says she told him she was actually Francesca's Personal Assistant, but I don't know what she assists her with. I think she's really the general office dogsbody...apart from you, Ellie, but as you're not permanent staff she'll only have you to boss about for a couple of weeks. Poor Carlotta!"

"There was a man in Angel's office," remembered Ellie. "I think Flynn said his name was Joe."

"Oh yes." Sophie smiled. "That's Joe Eagle. He's okay. He's the freelance photographer they use a lot and a very straight up and down sort of guy. Don't expect him to be your best buddy, but he won't be horrible to you either. He's a family man. He isn't interested in all the backbiting that goes on. And that's everyone you need to know about in that office," she finished, looking pretty pleased with herself. "You'll come into contact with staff in the other departments if you're here long enough, but I think that's enough new people to cope with for one day."

"Except for you," said Ellie. "Why are you working here if most people are so horrible?"

"Well..." Sophie shuddered. "I wouldn't want to be employed in Angel's office." She pulled a face. "Or in any of the other departments to be honest. It's great down here though. It's almost like not having a boss, because everyone leaves me pretty much alone. And it's convenient, because Flynn and I can come into work together in his car. And down here I miss most of the infighting. Besides, I'm only doing it until I can make it as a potter."

"You make pots?"

Sophie nodded. "It was my thing at art college, but it's hard to make a living creating studio pottery. Most people end up making domestic stuff, like mugs and bowls that are designed for everyday use, but I want to be taken seriously as an artist. I want to make stuff that is collected for its own sake, because people think it's beautiful." She pointed to a tall, elegant pot, resting on a shelf behind her. "This is one of mine. I keep it here in case anyone comes in who might be useful to my career. It hasn't happened yet, but you never know!"

"Wow!" Ellie gazed at the beautiful pot with its deep green glaze. The colour made her think of a shadowy pool of cool water. "It's lovely."

"Thank you," said Sophie, looking pleased. "So we both have big ambitions. You want to write world-famous articles, and I want to create world-famous pots. Not too big an ask, is it?"

Sophie smiled, and Ellie smiled back. They *were* big ambitions, but Ellie had begun the first faltering steps towards becoming a journalist. Thanks to Uncle Patrick she was here, at the *Heart* offices. Now, she was determined to prove that she had the makings of the sort of brilliant writer a magazine like *Heart* would be willing to *kill* for.

3
An amazing chance

Ellie's first day had been difficult, but buoyed up by Sophie's friendship she arrived the next morning determined to get as much as she could out of her work experience – and to enjoy it too. For a start she had brought a pair of her own shoes, with more manageable heels. She changed out of her boots thinking that, already, today was better than the previous one. She might not feel exactly welcome, but she was getting familiar with the office, and now she at least knew who everyone was.

She was greeted with a bit of good news. Flynn had found her a laptop. "Can I set it up at the far end of the reception desk?" Flynn asked Carlotta.

Carlotta nodded. "I'll just make some room."

She picked up a huge, flowering plant in its white china bowl and put it on a low table. Then she opened one of the drawers in the desk and scooped out a collection of pens, stray paperclips and a spare pair of tights. "There you are," she said to Ellie. "You can have that drawer for your things. Keep the top of the desk tidy, or Angel will go ballistic." She looked disparagingly at the laptop. "Pity it's so ancient," she said to Flynn. "Couldn't you find something that looks a bit smarter? After all, this is our front desk."

Flynn grinned. "It's only a couple of years old. And I'm sure any visitors will be far too busy looking at your welcoming smile to notice Ellie's computer." He turned to Ellie. "Now, Ellie. You need to set a password to get into the system. Key it in there, but don't let me, or anyone else, know what it is. Okay?"

"That's great. Thanks!"

Ellie settled herself into her own space once Flynn had gone, feeling almost like a real journalist. She tucked her bag neatly out of sight and put her pen in the drawer. The pen sounded a bit sad, rattling away on its own as she closed the drawer, so she took it out again and put it next to her laptop. She looked at Carlotta, to share a smile, but the receptionist was working at something on her screen and didn't notice.

Ellie's seat had height adjustment, so she spent a couple of minutes making sure it was in the right position. She was looking forward to being asked to try writing something, but everyone seemed too busy to give her any job at all.

She decided to fill in time by writing about what it was like to be in the *Heart* office for her school report, but before she could make a start, Piano came over to the reception desk.

"Angel's coffee," she said, and strode impressively away in her high heels without waiting for an answer.

Carlotta looked at her watch. "Okay. So here's what you do," she explained to Ellie. "Angel likes her first coffee in about half an hour, so you'll need to go in a minute because there can be a queue."

Ellie looked at the vending machine in the lobby. "A queue?"

Carlotta followed her gaze and laughed. "Oh no! We go to Coffee! Coffee! in the High Street." She shuddered. "We *never* have vending machine coffee. In fact..." She smiled brightly at Ellie. "While you're out you could bring me one too."

Thanks to Angel's demands for almost non-stop caffeine – and Carlotta's determination that Ellie should relieve her of the job of fetching it – she soon knew where the nearest coffee shop was, and even if this was to be her entire work experience, at least she was pleased to be busy!

By midday, she had fetched coffee for everyone, and got the order correct; she had unpacked a huge box of handbags with Sophie and carried them up to the office for Angel to consider; and she'd reported to Carlotta that the water cooler was empty.

"Tell Piano," said Carlotta, who was busy keying something into her computer.

Piano made Ellie wait by her desk like a naughty schoolgirl until she'd finished what she was doing. Then she listened impatiently. "The water company's pathetic," she said, glaring at Ellie as if it was her fault. "They never deliver in time. We'll have to find a different supplier." She went over to Francesca's desk and Ellie looked up to see Sophie, carrying an armful of post.

55

Ellie would have liked to chat, but it was obvious that Sophie was in a hurry. She handed the post to Carlotta and gave Ellie a quick grin. "Catch you later," she muttered as she left the office and collected her loaded post trolley, which she'd left in the lobby.

Ellie tried to ignore the way Piano irritated her by acting so superior, and turned her attention to her bit of desk space, which had just become hidden under the pile of post. Carlotta had dumped the lot in front of Ellie's laptop.

"What do you want me to do with all this?" Ellie asked.

Carlotta shrugged. "Open it."

Ellie sat down and started sorting through the envelopes. Actually, the discarded post proved to be rather interesting. One package was from a record company that was trying to promote an up-and-coming new band. Ellie studied the glossy photograph of the four boys and one girl who made up the band – which was called, Calumny. The girl was holding a bass guitar and glowering under her cropped hair. Three of the boys looked equally straight-faced and edgy, but the fourth, a blond-headed, good-looking boy, who clutched an electric violin, hadn't been able to hide the glimmer of an excited smile. Ellie found herself smiling back at him. He couldn't help looking thrilled at having made it this far, and Ellie could imagine just how he felt.

Ellie threw away the packaging, and made a neat pile of the photograph, CD and publicity flyer, as well as the covering letter. She wondered if the band would get any publicity in *Heart*. Maybe she'd ask if she could have the CD if no one else wanted it. If she liked the sound she could give the band a bit of exposure at school.

Once her desk was tidy again, Francesca called her over.

"Bring your notebook and come into Angel's office," she said. "Angel's going out, and there's something we need to discuss. It'll be quieter in there."

"But I don't have a notebook."

Francesca didn't hear, or maybe she wasn't interested. "Hurry up."

Ellie grabbed her bag and followed. She knew she had a pen in there, and...what about the old black notebook of her dad's that Mum had given her? Ellie had taken it out of her bag a couple of times at home, and turned it over in her hands, not sure what to do with it. The old-fashioned notebook was held closed with an elastic strap, and somehow she hadn't felt like opening it. Mum had told her that it was unused but, in spite of this, Ellie wasn't sure that she wanted to write in it. Closed, it was like some sort of secret. Open, she was afraid it might become just any old uncool notebook with yellowing paper. In the end she'd kept it in her bag, but more as a good-luck charm from her long-dead father than anything else.

Ellie hurried to keep up with Francesca. She couldn't think of anything she'd done wrong, but whenever any of the staff spoke to her she got the feeling she was going to be told off. She sidled up to the door, but, to her relief, Angel came out as she was about to go in.

"Don't make a mess in my office," she said imperiously. "I know what you young girls are like."

Ellie bit back a retort. It was obvious Angel didn't know what *she* was like. Ellie went in to find Francesca already perched elegantly on the edge of Angel's vast desk.

"Sit down."

Ellie chose one of the soft blue chairs Angel kept for her guests rather than the long, white leather sofa, and rummaged in her bag.

"Ready?"

"Yes...I'm...just looking for my notebook."
Ellie pulled the scruffy black book out of her
bag and put it on her knee.

"Good." Francesca sounded amused.

"It was my dad's," said Ellie, in case
Francesca thought it had been her own choice.

"Really?" Francesca stopped sounding
amused and looked interested. "Your father
was Daniel Ixos, wasn't he?"

Ellie was surprised that Francesca had
heard of him. "Yes."

"I've read some of his work." Francesca
sounded enthusiastic. "He was a great
journalist... How wonderful to have one of his
notebooks. May I see?"

Ellie passed the notebook to Francesca. She
turned it over in her hands, without undoing
the band of elastic. She smiled encouragingly
at Ellie as she handed it back. "Maybe it'll bring
you luck."

"I hope so," said Ellie.

There was silence for a moment, and then Francesca cleared her throat. "Angel wondered, now that you're settled in, if you'd like to try your hand at writing an article for us?"

Ellie's eyes widened with excitement. "Yes please!"

Francesca held up a warning hand. "Now don't get too carried away. For us to actually publish it, it would have to be of a very high standard. But because you're the age of our readers it might be fun to see what you can do. And if it has promise, one of us can always polish it up when you've written it."

Inwardly, Ellie bridled at the suggestion that anyone might have to polish up something she might write, but she tried to keep an even expression on her face. "So...what would you like me to write about?" she said, excitement bubbling up inside her.

"Well." Francesca folded her arms. "We have an interview coming up with Pop and Lolly

Lowther. You're about the same age as they were when they recorded their first hit single, so it might be interesting if you did the interview and then tried your hand at writing the feature."

Ellie stared at Francesca. For a moment she wasn't sure if she'd heard correctly. "Interview Pop and Lolly Lowther? Wow! That's fantastic!"

Ellie's brain was reeling. She had hoped to be able to do a write-up on something... perfume, or handbags...or, best of all, an in-depth piece about an animal sanctuary maybe, or global warming. But to interview the famous pop singer twins and then write a feature about them... Could she make the leap from school magazine contributor to this without making a fool of herself? Even as she wavered, she knew that no way was she going to turn down this chance.

Francesca was still talking. "You can't write

any of this down unless you open your notebook." She was looking amused again. Ellie fumbled with the elastic and pushed back the cover with trembling fingers. On the first page, written in pencil were the words *You can do this!*

Ellie froze, her pen hovering uncertainly above the page. It was as if the ghost of her dad was sitting in the room with her, urging her on. And yet he must have written this before Ellie was born, just before he'd set out on that last fateful journey. Why had he written those particular words? Surely he was a really confident, experienced journalist? She decided to ask her mum what she thought. Meanwhile, she couldn't sit here dreaming. Ellie took a deep breath. Yes, she *could* do this interview, or at least, she was determined to try her best. She tuned in to what Francesca was saying, and started scribbling madly below her father's words.

<u>Research</u>
Old school, fashion shoots, cuttings,
internet, ask Piano for help!!
First recording, favourite fashion labels,
check old issues.
Have we interviewed them before?
Yes?? Year before last Fr thinks.

"The other thing you'll need to do is to trawl through some of our old issues to research what sort of questions our readers like us to ask," continued Francesca. "In fact, do that first. It'll inform the research you do about the Lowthers."

"Um…"

"Yes?"

"I already know what sort of questions readers like," said Ellie, proudly, suddenly feeling more confident. "I read the magazine every month without fail."

Francesca smiled. "Do it anyway," she said. "Don't make assumptions. If you do you'll make mistakes. Off you go then."

"But…"

Francesca looked at her and raised her eyebrows.

"When is the interview going to happen?" asked Ellie.

"Oh yes. Good question. It's scheduled for the day after tomorrow, here, at two-thirty." She gave Ellie an appraising glance. "And don't try to dress too grown-up. We want you to look your age for the photographs. There's no point in someone of our readers' age conducting the interview unless the readers can see you doing it."

Somehow, Ellie stumbled out of the office. From fetching and carrying she had suddenly gone to interviewing mega-famous pop stars. Wow! And apparently she would be in the pictures as well. *Double* wow! But there was no time to daydream. She needed to get on with her research right away!

What to wear?

As Ellie headed towards her place at the reception desk, feeling as if her feet were hardly touching the floor, she was very aware that Piano was looking at her suspiciously. Ellie tried to rearrange her expression, so she didn't look quite as excited as she felt, but it wasn't easy. As soon as she reached her chair she plonked herself down and opened her laptop, keen to get on with some Pop and Lolly research.

"What did she want then?" said Carlotta.

Ellie turned eagerly to her. "Angel's going to let me interview Pop and Lolly Lowther, and then try to write a feature on them. Isn't that exciting? I hope I can manage…" Ellie stumbled to a halt as she noticed Carlotta's face change from mild interest, through confusion, to hurt and then to anger. Ellie remembered that Carlotta had been hoping for some more writing work herself. No wonder she was upset.

"But…I bet I make a hash of it," Ellie gabbled, trying to limit the hurt she had unwittingly inflicted on Carlotta. "They probably won't be here for more than five minutes…and I don't suppose my article will be any good… Sorry," she ended, feeling terrible. "I think it's just because I'm so young…" She was only making things worse.

Carlotta stared at her for what seemed like hours, and then turned away, tight lipped. She didn't speak to Ellie again for the rest of the day.

Over the next twenty-four hours, in between running errands for the rest of the staff, Ellie worked really hard on her assignment. From being underemployed she suddenly had far too much to do. Every time Angel strode through the office, Ellie learned to make herself as small as possible, and to keep her head down. If Angel noticed her she was likely to send her for coffee or give her Ferdinand's lead and tell her to take him out for an hour. Ellie did as she was asked without protest, but as soon as she had a moment to herself she would be back, immersing herself in research about Pop and Lolly Lowther, the model and singer twins who had started modelling when they were only toddlers, and were Ellie's age when they recorded their first pop song. They were doing the interview because now they'd recently left school, Lolly was intending to go to university, while Pop had decided to launch herself as a solo artist. Ellie couldn't *wait* to meet them.

And although Carlotta was taking time to get over her disappointment, Ellie found she had a new ally. Francesca had happened to overhear Piano telling Ellie to clear out the stationery cupboard and she'd intervened.

"That can wait," she'd said mildly, though both Piano and Ellie were left in no doubt that she'd meant every word. "Ellie is working."

Piano shot Ellie a poisonous look, but didn't say anything. Ellie was discovering just what a peach of a job the others considered the interview to be, and how jealous they were, but she didn't care. This was her chance to prove herself, and she wasn't going to let Piano, Carlotta, or anyone else put her off.

There was plenty about Pop and Lolly on the internet. Ellie turned from the laptop screen to her notes. She had a question she needed to write down: had Lolly's decision to study medicine been an easy one? It would be interesting to know why she wanted to change her career so dramatically. There was a world of difference between being a celebrity performer and a medical student.

Ellie had printed out a list of questions that were regularly used by *Heart* interviewers, but she saw no reason why she couldn't ask one or two of her own. After all, you couldn't call yourself a journalist unless you were prepared to probe. A shiver of expectation ruffled the fine little hairs on Ellie's arms. She hoped she wouldn't be totally cowed by such a high-profile interview when the time came. What if she messed it up?

Back home after work, Ellie thumbed through her notebook, reading over her notes for the interview the following day. Seeing her father's words again, she remembered about showing her mum and went to find her.

Georgia and Ellie sat at the kitchen table together to look at the book. "That's amazing," said Georgia quietly, as she read the words her husband had written over fourteen years ago. "I had no idea. I realized he hadn't taken it with him, and just assumed there wasn't anything in it."

"What I don't understand is why he wrote *You can do this!*" said Ellie. "It means a lot to me, because I'm just starting out, and need all the encouragement I can get. But he was really experienced."

Georgia had a faraway look in her eye. "Experienced, yes," she said. "But, though he never said anything to me about it, I knew how much he had to psych himself up for those trips. He wasn't an irresponsible thrill seeker. He went to those dangerous places because he thought he owed it to the people who had died there. He wanted their stories to be told." Georgia touched the pencilled words gently with her finger. "I wish I'd known about this before. I'd have been more understanding that last time he went away. I was expecting you at the time. I didn't want him to go. I didn't make it easy for him."

Ellie bit her lip. "Maybe I shouldn't have shown you," she said.

Georgia shook her head. "No. You did the right thing. Really. Did he write anything else?"

Ellie thumbed through. There seemed to be a phrase at the top of every few pages. Ellie's heart beat faster. The second phrase, five pages in, was *Trust your instincts*. Ten pages in, the third phrase was *Make someone smile every day*. She showed her mum.

"He used to say that to me all the time," said Georgia. "Needless to say, we didn't always manage it!"

Ellie felt overwhelmed with emotion. She had never met her dad, and yet he was speaking to her, using phrases that obviously had meant something important to him.

"I don't think I want to read any more just now," she said to her mum. "You can if you like, but I think, if there are any more I'll save them for later. He must have spaced them out through the notebook so he could savour each one as he reached it. I think I'll do the same."

Georgia gave her daughter a hug. "Your dad would have approved of that," she said admiringly. "I would never have the self-discipline to do the same, but it's a very good plan."

After supper, Ellie had to decide what she was going to wear for the interview. She tried to view her wardrobe dispassionately. What she saw didn't impress her. She'd always been happy enough with her clothes in the past. She had loads of T-shirts and tops, several skirts and a couple of pairs of decent jeans – but since she'd started at *Heart*, dissatisfaction had crept in. It wasn't that Ellie wanted to try to emulate Angel or Francesca. They were virtually stellar in the fashion stakes, but were much older than her, and their clothes didn't appeal to Ellie. But Carlotta and Piano had the sort of style that made her despair. It wasn't so much that their clothes were expensive, though it was obvious that some of them were. It was more that, whilst Ellie had always thought she looked fine, next to Carlotta and Piano – and with such famous people to interview – she suddenly felt totally uncool.

"What are you doing?" Ellie's mum was standing in the doorway, looking at the heap of discarded clothes on Ellie's bed.

"Trying to decide what to wear tomorrow." Ellie tried not to let her voice seem plaintive, but even to her own ears it sounded suspiciously like muted wailing.

"Didn't you borrow something from *Heart*?"

Ellie frowned. "What do you mean?"

Georgia smiled. "Aren't there racks of samples everywhere? I thought that was what it was like in these fashion magazines."

Ellie's face fell. "There *are* loads of

samples," she admitted. "But it didn't occur to me to ask if I could borrow anything, and it's too late now!"

Ellie's mum smiled. "It doesn't matter," she said. "You'll know next time. For now, what about your new cream top and jeans?"

Ellie gave her a pitying look.

Her mum soldiered on. "Jeans are cool. And your new top suits you."

Ellie plonked herself down amongst the clothes and folded her arms, feeling furious. "I bet we *are* allowed to borrow stuff. Piano and Carlotta are always turning up in new things but complaining about their low wages. I'm so stupid! Why didn't I realize?" Ellie was really annoyed with herself, but she was even more angry with the girls in the office. *Someone* could have helped her out. Carlotta and Piano probably hadn't because they were still jealous she'd got the assignment. Still, feeling sorry for herself wasn't going to make things any better. She needed inspiration, and she needed it *now*.

"I'm not trying to be funny, Mum," she said. "But I am going to be interviewing Pop and Lolly Lowther. I'll feel invisible next to them unless I wear something special...and I don't have anything even approaching special."

Georgia Ixos moved some of the clothes aside and joined her daughter on the bed. "I know what you mean, love. But will they be wearing glamorous clothes for an interview?"

Ellie shrugged. "I don't know. But they used to be models as well. So probably."

"Shouldn't a good interviewer be almost invisible?"

Ellie considered. "Well, maybe," she admitted, trying to be fair. "But they are only letting me do this particular job because of my age. And it's not just the interview. They are going to take pictures!" Ellie leaned her elbows on her knees and put her chin in her hands.

"All my friends will buy the magazine to see me in it...and I'll look pathetic!" All of a sudden she felt tears pricking at the backs of her eyes.

Georgia put her arm round her daughter and hugged her. "There's no way you'll look pathetic. But I do understand, love – feeling it is just as bad as looking it, when you're in a situation like that."

"I've been through everything I've got, Mum," Ellie mumbled into her hands. "And it's hopeless."

"What about a retro look?"

Ellie sank down backwards, until she lay amongst the disorder from her wardrobe. "I don't have anything retro," she said.

"I do," said Georgia in a quiet voice.

Ellie's reply was muffled by clothing. "What?"

"There's Granny's sixties daisy dress."

Ellie fought to sit up again and emerged with her hair in a mess. "What daisy dress?"

Georgia smiled. "I don't think you've ever seen it. It was never right for any of the fancy-dress parties you've been to. And it's so pretty I could never bring myself to put it in the dressing-up box for you when you were little. I was afraid it might get torn. It's in a bag in my wardrobe. Would you like me to get it?"

Ellie looked uncertain. "Okay."

While her mum went to find it, Ellie tried not to hope too much. It was almost certain to be dire. Retro clothes could be cool, but that didn't mean *anything* old would work, and the sixties had started over fifty years ago! Could *any* clothes last that long and still look good? Her mum was gone for quite a long time, and when she finally returned, Ellie was busy folding up tops and shoving them back where they belonged. She had put aside a skinny top to wear. It meant she would probably be cold during the interview, but it would be worth it not to feel a total loser. It would just about do, paired with her best jeans.

"Here you are! Sorry I was so long. I'd forgotten where I'd put it. Anyway, it needs ironing, but see what you think." Her mum held out a plastic carrier bag in one hand and some sort of hat in the other.

Ellie took the bag, and gave the hat a baleful glance. "You know I don't wear hats."

Slowly, she drew a handful of dark blue fabric out of the bag. It felt limp and was badly creased, but, actually, now she could see, it wasn't just blue, it was dotted with huge, white, abstract daisies with bright pink centres. The design should have been awful, but strangely it wasn't. She shook the dress out and stood up. The long sleeves were tapered in tightly at the wrist, and there was a wide belt covered in the same fabric to cinch in her waist. It had a high neck and a short, flared skirt that would swirl about as she walked. It looked different from anything Ellie had ever worn before.

Georgia opened the wardrobe door so that Ellie could look at herself in the long mirror. She held the dress up against her front and looked. "I'm not sure. It's…" Ellie couldn't imagine her granny ever wearing this dress. It was too funky. It shouted hot summer days and noisy parties. It was somehow wild and yet demure at the same time. "Maybe if we ironed it…"

"Don't go away. I'll do it. It'll only take a couple of minutes." Georgia grabbed the dress, and Ellie could hear her mum setting up the ironing board in the kitchen. Ellie felt she should offer to do it. After all, it was for her, but instead she waited, trying not to expect too much.

"Try it on."

Ellie scrambled into the dress. It felt strange. The cut was so different to the clothes she was used to.

"Put on your sandals," said her mum.

"Before you look at yourself again."

As Ellie stood up in her low-heeled sandals, her mum plonked something on her head.

"This was Granny's too. She used to have a thing about John Lennon. You know? From the Beatles." The cap had gone on at an angle, and Ellie shook her head in irritation. "I hate hats!" But before she could wrench it off her head she caught a glimpse of herself in the mirror.

Suddenly it wasn't Ellie Ixos standing in front of the wardrobe mirror, with a grumpy expression on her face. Instead, there was a person with real style, with the sort of edginess she'd admired in Carlotta and Piano. It wasn't up-to-the-minute fashion, but it worked in a way none of her clothes had ever worked before. The modern shoes with the retro dress and, most of all – though she hated to admit it – the cap: that was what pulled it all together and turned the outfit into something special. She didn't know *why* it looked so totally cool, instead of like a nerdy fancy-dress outfit, but she did know, beyond anything she'd known before, that it worked.

5

The interview

The morning of the interview, Ellie got up very early. She was ready ages before she needed to be and sat in her room, wondering how to stop herself getting even more horribly nervous. To distract herself, she decided to see if her best friend, Hannah, was online. She wasn't, so Ellie wrote her a message on Facebook: *So nervous about interviewing Pop and Lolly Lowther today. Wish me luck! I'll be online again at the end of the day. Watch this space...*

She read over what she'd written and paused. What if the interview went disastrously wrong? She wouldn't feel like chatting about it then. Maybe she ought to delete the last bit.

83

But before she could do anything about it her mobile rang. It was Hannah.

"Thought I'd ring to say good luck," said Hannah, "before I get on the Tube."

"Thanks," said Ellie. "I was going to leave you a message on Facebook. I thought you might have forgotten about the interview."

"No way!" said Hannah, sounding affronted. "As if I would."

"Sorry," said Ellie. "I'm just so nervous! What are you up to today?"

"We've got a nursery school group coming in, so I'll probably spend all my time trying to stop the children hugging the chicks to death," said Hannah with a laugh. "Working at a city farm isn't exactly glamorous like your job."

"But you love it," said Ellie.

"Yes," said Hannah. "I do."

By the time Ellie and Hannah had stopped chatting it was time to go. In fact Ellie had to hurry. She was just in time to catch the bus and slumped into her seat with a sigh of relief. She pulled out her notebook and studied the questions she'd prepared. She wanted to feel as much in control as possible. She also reread her dad's second phrase. *Trust your instincts.* She planned on doing that too.

As soon as she reached the office she hung up her coat, and put on her sandals. It felt odd to be keeping the cap on indoors, but that was probably because she wasn't used to wearing any kind of hat, indoors or out.

She was a few minutes early, and so instead of going straight into the office she headed downstairs to see Sophie. Ellie hoped she'd be able to tell from Sophie's expression if the outfit worked or not. She had been so certain last night that the retro look was brilliant, but now she was starting to doubt it, and she needed some extra reassurance. She needn't have worried.

"Wow! Get you!"

"Is it okay? Really?"

"Don't be an idiot!" Sophie rolled her eyes. "Of course it's okay! You look brilliant, better than any of the dragons upstairs. They'd better watch out or the Fashion Department will grab you."

Ellie beamed. "Thanks!"

"You got all your questions sorted?"

Ellie patted her bag. "In my notebook. I'd better go. Angel will be wanting her first order of coffee."

"Ellie."

"Yes?"

Sophie looked serious. "Just don't expect any compliments from them. You'll be lucky if you even get a raised eyebrow. But they'll notice how funky you look. Believe me."

Sophie was right. When Ellie went in, no one said a word. Piano might have pouted a little harder than usual, but Carlotta avoided having to greet her by looking away. Ellie couldn't detect anything that betrayed Angel's feelings about the sixties dress either, but she was sure that when Francesca came over to give her the morning coffee order, a slight ghost of a smile touched her lips...for an instant.

And no one was about to treat Ellie any differently, just because she had a high profile interview to conduct after lunch. If anything, they worked her harder than ever. Piano dumped an enormous heap of tops on her desk that had to be hung up, ready for Angel to look at, and then Carlotta disappeared off somewhere, leaving Ellie to man the reception desk, which she wasn't really supposed to do. After that, Angel told Piano to take Ferdinand for his walk, but as soon as the Editor started talking to Francesca about the next issue of the magazine, Piano handed Ellie the lead.

When Ellie and Ferdinand returned, the office seemed unbearably noisy, with conversations and people coming and going.

Usually Ellie liked it that way, but today, even when she had a few minutes to herself, she was finding it impossible to focus. She was just reading over the background notes she had made about the Lowthers, when Piano stomped up to Francesca's desk. Ellie found it impossible to tune out Piano's strident complaints. She watched the exchange with a carefully lowered head, in case someone noticed her and gave her another job to do.

"There's still no water in the cooler," Piano moaned. "I thought it was company policy for us to have it."

Francesca was deeply involved with an article she was writing, and didn't even look up. "So research a new supplier," she snapped.

"I can't do it now," said Piano. "I have to take a parcel downstairs to the post room. And anyway, I don't have the authority to order more, or cancel the—"

Francesca glanced up and glared at Piano.

"Ellie, get me the number will you? *I'll* cancel our present order, Piano, and when you come back you can research a new supplier for me."

Ellie sighed. She found the number from the database on her laptop, then went back and dialled it on Francesca's phone. As soon as she heard it ring, Ellie handed the phone to the Deputy Editor and went back to her notes. But no sooner had Francesca taken the receiver, than Carlotta arrived with an urgent message for her. Ellie felt like putting her hands over her ears. She watched Francesca trying to speak on the phone and listen to Carlotta whilst at the same time keeping track of the article she was writing. At that moment, Ellie didn't envy Francesca for her job one bit.

By lunchtime, Ellie had spent so much of the morning scurrying about on errands that she was exhausted. Usually, she took her sandwich downstairs and ate with Sophie and Flynn, but today there simply wasn't time.

Instead she grabbed a coffee from the vending machine that the others hardly ever used and sat down to gather her thoughts.

"Are you ready?" said Francesca. "The Lowthers will be here in a few minutes."

Ellie bit back a squeak of panic and rummaged in her bag for her notebook. Joe, the photographer, arrived and she felt her panic level rising. She wanted to go and check her make-up, but Francesca was watching her, so she opened her notebook instead. The writing was a blur. She couldn't take anything in, and she couldn't for the life of her remember what she had decided to say as an opener.

Then the Lowthers were there, at the reception desk, with Carlotta simpering away for all she was worth. One of the girls was wearing perfectly cut black jeans, with a loose printed top. The other was wearing a short dress, opaque tights and amazing short brown boots with gold heels. Ellie noticed that no one asked *them* to change out of their outdoor footwear!

The Lowthers were equally glamorous, just like the pictures she'd seen of them. And they really *were* identical. Thank goodness they were wearing different clothes, otherwise she'd *never* have been able to tell which one she was speaking to.

Was she supposed to go and greet them? No. Francesca was doing that, as poised as ever, shaking hands and showing them to the meeting room. As they passed Ellie's desk, Francesca glanced at her, and she remembered what she was supposed to do. She had to follow them and wait outside while Angel chatted to the guests for a few minutes. Then Angel would leave, Francesca would introduce Ellie to them, and leave them with Joe to do the photo shoot. After that, Ellie would have no more than twenty minutes to interview them. As she'd been told, she hurried over and loitered by the door.

"Ah, Ellie. There you are," said Francesca, emerging from the room a few minutes later. "Let me introduce you to Pop and Lolly Lowther."

The Lowthers were tall, very nearly as tall as Francesca, and Ellie discovered that even close up they still looked pretty well identical. Hopefully she'd remember which was gold heels, and which was black jeans.

The twins' faces seemed flawless, as if carved in a pale, coffee-coloured stone. But as soon as they spoke, their faces came alive, and Ellie reminded herself that, however extraordinary they were, Pop and Lolly were still just human beings, and she shouldn't allow herself to be overawed.

"Hi! I'm Pop," said one of the girls. She smiled as she held out her hand and Ellie shook it. She tried to fix in her mind that gold heels was Pop.

"And I'm Lolly," said black jeans, also shaking Ellie's hand. "I hear you're on work experience. I hope you're enjoying it."

Pop followed her sister's comment without allowing Ellie to reply. "You've managed to wangle this interview, which is quite an achievement I should think!" She grinned at Ellie and Ellie found herself grinning back. Everything was going to be all right.

It was great fun being photographed with the Lowther twins. They made it very easy for Joe, seeming to know exactly what he wanted almost before he spoke. But then, they had been photographed so many times since they were young children that it must be second nature for them by now.

Joe wanted to take some pictures of Ellie interviewing the twins, so Ellie opened her notebook and put on an enquiring expression, while both the Lowthers paid her a flattering amount of attention.

The time flew by, and after what seemed a very few minutes Joe had gone. "Well," said one of the twins – Ellie had somehow for the moment forgotten which was which. "Now it's just us. What do you want to know?"

"Don't worry," said the other kindly. She seemed to have sensed Ellie's sudden panic. "There are loads of stock questions that magazines always ask us. We can help you out if you like. Don't feel pressured."

"It's okay," said Ellie, finding her voice. "I've got my questions written down. All I have to do is run through them, if that's okay."

The twins sat together on a comfortable leather sofa, while Ellie took one of the blue chairs. They answered everything they could about their coming tour. Then they answered questions about their careers, their schooling at Rockley Park – the famous school for musically talented children – and their home life. Ellie was amazed to hear that they really had started their modelling career as infants! The student twin, Lolly, told Ellie a bit about the work she hoped eventually to do in India, where their mother's family came from, and Ellie remembered the special question that she wanted to ask.

"Why have you decided to give up your career with your sister to become a doctor?" she asked.

"I've been asked before about why I've decided to stop being a model and pop singer," said Lolly thoughtfully. "But I haven't seen the proper answer printed anywhere."

"Well, no magazine is going to print that you think being a pop singer is silly," laughed Pop.

"Do you really think that?" asked Ellie, feeling rather shocked.

"I don't think it's silly!" protested Lolly. "Otherwise I wouldn't be going on this tour, would I? No. There's nothing at all wrong with using your talent to be an entertainer. I just don't find it satisfies *me* somehow. I don't know why."

"She's always wanted to be a doctor really," said Pop, smiling affectionately at her sister. "And I was pretty cross about the idea of her deserting me at first." She grinned. "But she has to follow her heart, just as I do, and she is very clever."

"Ssh!" said Lolly, nudging her twin. "You're embarrassing me. And I still have to get a good degree. What if I flunk my exams?"

Pop rolled her eyes, and Ellie found herself giggling. The twins were great to be with, and very easy to like.

"Look," said Pop to Ellie, nudging her sister back with a grin, "we ought to be giving you something exclusive for your article, so you can show the Editor how brilliant you are."

"Good idea!" said Lolly. "What shall we tell her that no one else knows?"

Ellie sat between them, hugging her notebook to her chest, hardly able to believe her luck.

"I know," said Pop. "You can have it

exclusively from me that I'm about to launch a totally new venture!"

"Put something in to the effect that you made us feel so relaxed that Poppy let it slip by mistake," said Lolly.

"Okay," said Ellie. "So..." she added breathlessly to Pop. "What *is* your new venture going to be?"

"Ah! Well unfortunately I can't actually tell you quite yet," said Pop. "There are still a couple of things to put in place. But it should be enough for *Heart* to say that something's happening. And if you hint that your magazine might be the first to announce what it will be... well, it'll hopefully keep people buying the magazine until they find out."

"That's what editors like." Lolly gave Ellie a lovely smile. "Don't worry. It's true. She really is going to launch a new venture, very soon."

"If you email my agent in about a month's time she should be able to explain," said Pop.

"I'll give her your name so she'll be expecting your message."

"But Ellie will have finished her work experience by then," said Lolly.

Pop frowned, but soon brightened again. "Well she can still give *Heart* the exclusive information," she said. "Make sure they pay you for it too," she said to Ellie with a wink.

It was time for them to go.

"I love your dress, by the way," said Pop to Ellie as Angel appeared at the door, with Carlotta and Piano lurking nearby to catch a last glimpse of the celebrities. Ellie felt herself go pink with pleasure at the compliment.

Under Angel's withering look, Carlotta backed away and resumed her place at the reception desk. Piano was still hovering, but neither Pop nor Lolly gave her a second glance. And to Ellie's great delight, the twins gave her a hug before they allowed Angel to whisk them away.

"Good luck in the future," said Lolly.

"Don't forget to email," added Pop.

As Piano saw the visitors out, Ellie went back to her desk, feeling as if she was drifting along on a cloud of total happiness. She sat down and opened her notebook, intent on adding to the information she already had, while the interview was fresh in her mind. She hadn't made anything like as many notes as she'd intended, although she was fairly confident that she'd done enough. But before she began she just had to sit and revel in her experience. It had been quite simply the most exciting time of her life!

Ambition

Ellie worked hard on her article and, thankfully, apart from sending her out twice on errands for Angel, Piano mostly left her in peace.

As for Carlotta, Ellie hadn't wanted to fall out with her, but reluctantly assumed that she'd lost her ally. However, to Ellie's delight, Carlotta seemed to have forgiven her and was ready to be friends again. She wanted to know all about the interview, and Ellie tried to tell her as much as possible, without giving the impression she was bragging. It was great not to be shunned, but Carlotta seemed to be happy to chat all day, whereas Ellie wanted to get on with her article. In the end, Ellie simply had to ask her politely to stop talking, so she could work.

As the receptionist turned away with a pout, Ellie sighed. Now Carlotta would probably hate her again. It was an awful lot easier dealing with Piano. Ellie might not like Angel's assistant, but at least she was consistent in treating Ellie as if she was some sort of pond life.

At one point, Francesca found time to come over and give her a bit of advice, which Ellie was most grateful for.

"Try hinting at the most exciting item at the beginning of your article, and then go into more detail about it towards the end. That's the way to keep your readers hooked," she said.

"Thanks, Francesca!" Ellie looked at the first sentence, and rewrote it.

I thought it was exciting enough to be photographed with two of my fave people, but Pop 'n' Lolly hinted that they would give me and Heart *an exclusive scoop too!*

By the end of the day Ellie was happy with

what she'd written. She had tried to answer most of the questions readers liked to ask, and had added a bit about Lolly's hopes for her medical career. At the end she'd mentioned Pop's new project, and tried to make it clear that *Heart* would be in a position to tell all when the time came.

"I'll read it through as soon as I can," said Francesca when Ellie described what she'd done.

Ellie pushed her notebook into her bag and got ready to leave. As she went through to change her shoes in the lobby she met Piano, who was coming back from an errand.

"Pop Lowther was having a good laugh earlier, wasn't she?" Piano said, kicking off her outdoor shoes.

"What do you mean?" asked Ellie.

"Well..." Piano slipped on a pair of brilliant blue court shoes with see-through heels and smiled. "Saying she liked your dress. What a joke!" She pushed past Ellie and sauntered back to the office. Ellie stared at her back, trying without success not to feel upset. She was still smarting when Carlotta came for her coat.

"I'm sorry I couldn't talk more to you today," Ellie apologized. "But I really had to get that article written while the interview was fresh in my mind."

Carlotta didn't smile back. "You've got so up yourself," she said. "It's pathetic."

Ellie was stung. "I'm sorry," she said, swallowing her anger. "I do realize how lucky I am. But I'll be out of here very soon, and I'm sure you'll get your chance then."

Carlotta looked even more angry. "Don't patronize me," she snapped. "And don't bank on that article of yours getting into the magazine. It won't."

Ellie couldn't help replying. "You don't know that!"

Carlotta sneered. "It's the photographs

Angel really wanted. She'll put them in and not bother with an article. Captions will do, and Piano or I will do those."

"Well it was fun meeting the Lowthers," said Ellie, determined to be positive in the face of Carlotta's spitefulness. "I wouldn't have missed it for the world."

"I suppose it would have been a big thrill for *you*," said Carlotta pityingly, ignoring the fact that she'd wanted to hear all about it not long ago.

Ellie couldn't bring herself to reply. She flung on her coat and hurried off to catch the bus.

"Hey!" called Sophie, running to catch her up before she could reach the front entrance. "Come on! Tell all. Was it fabulous?" One look at Ellie's face was all Sophie needed. She put her arm round Ellie and drew her back into the lift and down into the basement. "Did it really go badly? I'm sure it was better than you think."

Ellie shrugged off Sophie's arm, thumped into a chair and folded her arms. "It was *brilliant*," she told Sophie, with a furious expression on her face. "The Lowthers were great, I remembered what to do, and I've finished the article. Thanks to a tip from Francesca I really think it's got a good chance of being published. I was feeling fantastic until Piano and Carlotta got their teeth into me. And I thought Carlotta *liked* me. Then she didn't for a bit, then she did, and now she doesn't again. It's crazy!"

Sophie sighed. "You just have to try and ignore them," she said. "I know they can be pretty poisonous, but it's only jealousy. They would *love* to be able to interview people instead of running errands for Angel, but all they get to do is make up readers' letters and make sure the horoscopes fit the available space."

Ellie sighed. "They can both be so... *horrible*." She gave Sophie a weak smile. "They don't *really* make up the readers' letters, do they?"

Sophie smiled back. "I invented that. I bet *Heart* gets loads of letters from readers, without Piano and Carlotta having to make them up. Let's go and see if Flynn has managed to get the car out of that shoebox they call a car park. We'll give you a lift home."

"But it's not on your way," said Ellie, feeling almost completely cheered up.

"Flynn won't mind. It looks like rain and we can't have our celebrity interviewer getting wet in the bus queue, can we?"

Flynn insisted on driving Ellie all the way home, and so Ellie invited them both in for a cup of tea. When Ellie's mum got in a few minutes later she found Ellie and two new faces sitting round the kitchen table, laughing happily together.

Ellie introduced them and poured her mum a mug of tea. In no time they were all listening to Ellie relive her day. Then Georgia wanted to know about Sophie's pots.

"If the company would only give me a rise, Soph could give up the post room job and be a full-time potter," said Flynn wistfully. "Instead of having to cram it into weekends and evenings."

Sophie put her arm round Flynn and gave him a kiss. "That's kind, but I don't mind," she said. "I have to make my pottery pay for itself. And you'll get a rise eventually. I'm sure you will."

Flynn grinned. "Either that, or you'll sell that pot you keep in the post room for a fortune to some celebrity who wanders down there by mistake. Then I won't have to work at all and you can keep me."

"You wish!" Sophie tried to look scandalized and failed dismally.

When Sophie and Flynn eventually left, Ellie and her mum waved them off and went

107

back into the kitchen to tidy up and start dinner.

"What lovely people," said Georgia, with her head in the fridge. "I feel a lot happier with you in that place knowing you have those two looking out for you. Sophie at least gives the impression that she has her feet firmly on the ground."

"And isn't Flynn good-looking?" said Ellie, stacking the mugs in the dishwasher.

Georgia withdrew her head and appeared with a selection of vegetables to chop. "He's obviously devoted to Sophie," she said primly. Then she looked at Ellie and grinned like a teenager. "And yes, he is totally gorgeous," she agreed. "But obviously taken, and much too old for you and much too young for me."

"Mum!"

There was silence for a few minutes while chopping got under way. Then Ellie cleared her throat. "Do you think Carlotta was right?

Will they dump my article and just print the pictures?"

Georgia stopped what she was doing and gave her daughter a hug. "I have no idea, love, but no one can take today away from you, can they? And it's all practice, isn't it? After all, I thought you wanted to be one of the best. That takes time."

"Yes," said Ellie thoughtfully. "Of course. I can't expect to breeze in there and become a brilliant journalist overnight. But it would be nice to see at least a *few* of my words in print."

Ellie resumed her chopping, thinking furiously. *Mum's right,* she thought. *I want to be a good journalist...the best I can be. And I've got Dad's words to spur me on. I don't care how horrible Piano and Carlotta are. I'm determined that eventually I can do this!*

7

Disaster

Friday went well, with Ellie feeling more settled and part of the Editorial Department, even though no other amazing jobs came her way. On Monday she breezed into work feeling on top of the world, but she arrived to find an awful atmosphere in the office. As she walked up to the reception desk, Carlotta gave her a very strange look. It seemed to Ellie to be a cross between pity and glee. Ellie found her heart beginning to thump and, as soon as Piano intercepted her, gripping her elbow in that spiteful way she had, Ellie knew she was in trouble.

"Angel wants to see you in her office. Now!"

Ellie wrenched her elbow free and scuttled to the Editor in Chief's closed door. She could feel Piano's venom – it almost seemed to be piercing her back as she went. She tried desperately to think of something, anything she might have done to bring this amount of anger in her direction. Apart from a week ago, when the Editor had referred to her as "it", Angel had hardly acknowledged Ellie's presence, and Piano simply ordered her about. What on earth could Angel want? Was it something about the interview with the Lowthers? Had they complained? But they'd seemed so happy with the way it had gone.

It was no good, she couldn't think of anything. She took a deep breath. She couldn't hang about any longer, with both Piano and Carlotta watching her. She simply had to knock on the door.

Ellie could make nothing out by the tone of voice Angel used to summon her. She opened the door, went in and was slightly relieved to find that Francesca was there as well. However, judging from Francesca's expression she wasn't ready to take Ellie's side any time soon.

Angel was holding Ferdinand under her arm as usual. She said nothing, but looked at Ellie as if she was the lowest form of life. She left Francesca to do the talking.

"A few minutes ago we took a call from Joe," Francesca told Ellie in a cold voice. "You know Joe, the photographer?"

Ellie found herself nodding quickly. "Yes, of course."

"He was scheduled to do a major shoot this morning with Sapphire, but she didn't turn up."

Ellie's face and mind went blank as she tried to work out what on earth a famous model not turning up for work had to do with her.

Francesca went on. "When we rang the agency to find out what the problem was we were told that *someone* had cancelled it on Thursday."

Ellie was waiting for Francesca to make it clear what any of this had to do with her, when Angel's voice cut across Francesca's as she stooped to put Ferdinand in his basket. "For goodness' sake, Francesca, get on with it... You! Whatsyourname, Ellie Ixos. What the hell did you think you were doing?"

Ellie's mouth dropped open and she hastily shut it again. "I...er..." She spread her hands in bewilderment. "I'm afraid I have no idea *who* might have done it. I was busy with the interview, and then the artic—"

"Never mind that! Are you deliberately trying to make trouble?"

Ellie took a deep breath of air into her lungs and tried to defend herself calmly. "No! I'm doing work experience. I just tidy up, and run errands – apart from the interview last week."

The sudden silence in the room was broken

only by Ferdinand scratching in his basket next to Angel's desk.

"I don't have time for this!" Angel waved a hand dismissively at them both. "And neither do you, Francesca. I expect you to run the office smoothly. Things like this should *not* happen."

Francesca's poise slipped a bit, and Ellie could tell that she was angry with her boss, but she didn't say anything.

Angel sat down behind her desk and pulled a sheaf of glossy photographs towards her. She spread them out on the desk before looking up at Francesca dismissively. "And I want ideas by lunchtime on how to fill the gap this blunder has left in next month's issue. Send Piano in. You're obviously too soft with the staff."

Francesca gave Ellie a little push and guided her out of the office. She closed the door behind them and led the way over to her desk. "Carlotta, you'll have to do the coffee run this morning," she said in a level voice. Carlotta had been lurking near the Editor's office, trying to look as if she might have some business being there. She pouted, then put her nose in the air and went to fetch her coat. Piano had rushed back to her desk as soon as Ellie and Francesca had appeared and was pretending to be exceptionally busy.

"Piano, Angel wants to see you in her office now," said Francesca. "We'll keep an eye on reception until Carlotta gets back. Now, Ellie..."

Ellie trembled under Francesca's intelligent gaze, but was determined to stick up for herself. It simply must have been one of the others who had made the call. But why would *anyone* working for *Heart* do such a thing?

"You do realize what a serious situation this is?" Francesca leaned against her desk and folded her arms. "We've now missed the opportunity of working with Sapphire for ages and, much worse, we have five blank pages to fill, and almost no time to do it."

"I do realize that it's awful," said Ellie hastily. "But why would anyone working here want to cancel a shoot?"

"That's what I can't understand," said Francesca.

"Well...are you sure it wasn't the model agency's fault?" said Ellie, thinking hard. "I mean, maybe someone took a message in their office from a different magazine and got it wrong. Maybe the mistake didn't happen here at all."

Francesca smiled slightly. "Ever thought of becoming a detective?"

Ellie blushed. "It just seems so unlikely that anyone here would have been responsible," she said. "What would be the point?"

"You're right," said Francesca. "Of course I thought that too. I'm sorry you were under suspicion, but Angel is going to tackle everyone in turn. You haven't been singled out. I expect she'll speak to Carlotta after Piano."

Francesca sighed. "The thing is that this is going to play hell with Angel's budget, and make her look sloppy. She might be in charge of *us*, but she still has to answer to the board, and she knows this mess isn't going to reflect well on her." She thought for a moment and then gave Ellie a smile. "I know, why don't you go and see if the post has come, and forget all about it. You like spending time with the post girl, don't you? And I need to get on with thinking about an alternative to fill the gap."

Ellie noticed how stressed Francesca looked. It must be difficult working closely with a boss as demanding as Angel. And it occurred to Ellie that Angel might well try to shift the blame onto her deputy. But there wasn't anything Ellie could do about that. She needed to worry about herself. She couldn't prove that she *hadn't* cancelled the shoot. What if Angel decided to tell her she wasn't allowed to finish her work experience? Everything had been going so well. The interview, and her article…was it all going to be wasted for a mistake some unknown person had made? If so, it was too unfair. Suddenly, Ellie felt totally out of place. She'd tried so hard to fit in, but really she knew she was seen as a nuisance at best. Piano would no doubt be feeling pretty bruised when she emerged from Angel's office, and the chances were that she'd vent her feelings on Ellie. Ellie didn't want to be on the receiving end of that. She hurried down to see Sophie, as Francesca had suggested.

The post hadn't come, but was due any minute, so Sophie put the kettle on and pulled a packet of biscuits out of a drawer labelled F. "It used to be labelled B," said Sophie, noticing Ellie's quizzical look. "But I decided F was better. It reminds me how Fat I'll get if I eat too many," she added as Ellie still looked puzzled.

Ellie laughed. "F could also mean Fillings in your teeth," she suggested.

"Even worse!" said Sophie, rolling her eyes. "So," she went on, ladling instant coffee granules into two mugs, "how's our grand celebrity interviewer today?"

"*I'm* all right," said Ellie. "But you'll never guess what's happened upstairs."

Ellie explained about the photo shoot, and Sophie looked serious. "Joe is in great demand," she told Ellie. "He's always said to Flynn how much he enjoys working for *Heart*, but if we start letting him down he might not want to any more. Jane in the Design Department told me that he's one of the best in the business – he can pretty well name his price. And another thing... Oh! Hang on, I'll just get that."

Ellie sipped her coffee while Sophie answered the phone. "...Not yet...no, well... I'll...here it is. I'll send it up. Bye."

The postman had arrived and was dumping

sacks of post by the counter, so Ellie helped Sophie to sort it. There was quite a lot for the Design Department, a load of letters for Ellie's office and a parcel for Angel, although it was addressed to Ferdinand.

"Typical!" said Sophie. "I bet it's another of those awful costumes she dresses him up in, the poor animal."

"I think he looks quite cute," giggled Ellie. "Did you see him in that pixie outfit? I'm sure he likes being the centre of attention."

"Huh! In my opinion dogs ought to be allowed to be dogs, not dressed up to look like people. Angel will be doing a feature on doggy fashion next."

Ellie picked up the letters and the offending parcel. "I'll deliver these for you," she offered. "Actually," she added, pausing at the door, "that's a great idea about doggy fashion. I'll mention it to Francesca. She's desperate for a filler."

"Don't you dare!"

Ellie gave Sophie a grin and disappeared back upstairs.

"You know, that actually *is* a great idea," said Francesca when Ellie mentioned it. "We could have a few pics of Ferdinand and ask readers to send in their own dressed-up pet pictures. We could even offer a prize for the best, chosen by Ferdinand – well, you know...Angel really – but we can say that Ferdinand had a paw in it." Francesca actually smiled another proper smile at Ellie.

"It was Sophie's idea," said Ellie, determined to be honest.

"But you thought to mention it," said Francesca, taking the parcel. "As long as we can get a suitable photographer, we should be able to have it done in time for the next issue and, as it's something to do with Ferdinand, hopefully Angel will go for it. Well done!"

Ellie watched Francesca make her way over to Angel's office with a warm glow of achievement. The day had begun disastrously, but now things were really looking up!

8

Competition time

For the rest of the morning Ellie tried to keep well away from Angel's office, in case she came out and harangued her again, but the Editor and her deputy were far too busy making sure that they had enough material for the next issue. They didn't even demand coffee for ages, but eventually Francesca put her head round the door and sent Ellie to get it. Once she had delivered their order, Francesca sent Ellie over to help Piano and Carlotta with the previous month's competition entries.

Heart ran a competition in most issues, and Ellie had sometimes entered them. Although she often had the right answers she'd never won, so she was very interested to find out how the winner was chosen.

Last month, readers had had to name the members of a new band that had been interviewed. All the names were actually in the article, but it was amazing how many incorrect entries had come in. Some readers had simply been careless, and spelled the name Scott with one "T". According to Piano, that meant they couldn't win, which Ellie thought was a bit harsh. But a few entries were so inaccurate it seemed that the article hadn't even been read! She found one entry that had only three names on it, while there were actually five members in the band.

Sorting out the correct entries from the ones with careless mistakes showed her how important it was to enter competitions carefully. She decided to double-check every last detail when she went in for competitions in future.

It made her feel quite special, checking

competition entries. It would be terrible if she made a mistake and put an entry in the wrong heap, so she took her time over it and, fortunately, no one disturbed her while she was busy.

But Ellie wasn't going to be allowed to choose the actual winner. As there were always a number of correct entries, the fairest way was to pull a name out of a hat. Apparently Piano always reserved that pleasure for herself. Ellie could tell that Carlotta would dearly have loved a turn, but, like Ellie, she had to do as she was told. Ellie shot her a sympathetic glance, wondering if their similar feelings would make Carlotta feel friendly towards her again, and Carlotta gave her a slight smile back. Ellie was relieved. Life was too short to stay annoyed with people, she thought, and she was pleased that Carlotta seemed to feel the same.

As soon as Ellie had sorted the entries into two piles, Piano grabbed the winning ones and put them into a large Top Shop handbag that she kept for the purpose. She handed the bag to Carlotta who shook it vigorously. Piano shut her eyes and turned away. She reached out, felt for the top of the bag, and rummaged about inside. Ellie tried not to feel hurt that she wasn't allowed to join in, but failed.

"Here you are," said Piano, handing Ellie the slip she had made such a show of picking out. "The prize is on my desk. Put it in a jiffy bag and try to address it properly. Use a *Heart* address label. Don't just scrawl on the bag. I wouldn't put that sort of thing past you."

The catty remark was all the more hurtful for being devastatingly accurate. Ellie had forgotten the magazine had its own printed labels. She blushed and tried to hide her confusion by scurrying off to fetch the prize. It was the band's first CD, one of their posters and a smaller, autographed photograph of them all.

When she came to pack the bag, Ellie noticed that Piano hadn't written on the compliment slip she was sending with the prize. While Piano wasn't looking, Ellie scribbled a note to the winner, feeling very daring. *Well done!* she wrote. *I hope you enjoy your prize. Watch out for the next competition. Just because you've won once, doesn't mean you can't win again!*

She was very tempted to add *From Ellie Ixos*, but thought that was probably going too far.

Happy with her small triumph over the others, Ellie packed up the prize, and took the parcel down to Sophie. It was nearly lunchtime, so she managed to have quite a long time away from the editorial office.

"Francesca loved your dressed-up animals – she thought it was a great idea," she told Sophie with a grin. "She's going to pitch it to Angel. Fashion shoot and competition."

"I didn't think you'd really mention it!"

Sophie sounded amused. "I don't know. Here we are with global warming and loads of animals almost extinct, and all our magazine can do is write articles about fancy-dress clothes for pets!"

"I wonder who *will* write the article," said Ellie.

"Francesca maybe?" suggested Sophie. "If she has time to do it. Or Piano. I bet she's good at silly and pointless articles."

"*I* could write a good article about it," said Ellie feeling wistful. "I'd have a picture of Ferdinand dressed as a pixie next to one of those awful charity photographs of neglected animals." She thought for a moment. "In my article I'd be asking why animal lovers are spending a fortune on stuff like that when they could be helping animals that really need it."

Sophie looked at Ellie. "You've got the sort of enquiring mind that will take you places," she said.

Ellie went pink with pleasure. "You think so?"

"Of course. You're full of ideas about everything that comes up. Let's face it, almost every subject under the sun has been written about at some time. Journalism is all about finding different angles to engage a reader's interest."

Ellie thought of her dad's words in the notebook. "One day," she said firmly. "Like you and your pots, Sophie." She tidied away the remains of her lunch and got up. "Well, I'd better go and see what the dragons have got for me to do this afternoon. See you later!"

Upstairs, everything was calm. Piano had a couple of Ferdinand's costumes on her desk and was making a start on an article. Carlotta was dealing with what sounded like a rather difficult person on the telephone and Francesca emerged from Angel's office looking the happiest she'd been all day.

"You said you'd done your article on the Lowthers, didn't you?"

Ellie nodded. "It's on the system in my folder," she said.

"I'll look at it now," said Francesca. "I've got a few minutes. Make sure you don't slope off anywhere until I've read it. Don't worry," she said, seeing the apprehensive expression on Ellie's face. "Piano can always rewrite the article if yours isn't quite up to our standard."

That wasn't what Ellie wanted to hear, but at least Francesca was going to read it. She might have insisted that Ellie and Piano wrote it together, without even giving her a chance to do it on her own.

While she waited for the verdict, Ellie unpacked a box of next season's T-shirts that had been sent up by the Fashion Department. They were going to be in a chain of high-street stores, and *Heart* would be reviewing them.

Piano drifted past and touched one of them with an immaculately polished nail.

"I wouldn't wear any of those, even if you *paid* me," she said grandly. "But I suppose the designer took Angel out for lunch." She sighed theatrically and glanced at Ellie.

Ellie thought about how useful a favourable review would be to the designer and the high-street stores. Maybe designers *did* buy Angel lunch from time to time, but Ellie couldn't imagine her being swayed by a meal. For the first time she realized how influential magazines could be. Ellie had never considered that she might be influenced by *Heart*, but she realized that every month she did take notice of articles and photographs, and she would quite often look out for something she'd seen in it. Magazines like *Heart* must be very important to shops and fashion designers. No wonder they tried hard to get into the pages as often as possible.

Ellie had never fancied being a model, but it was exciting to see the new ranges before they even went into the shops. She must remember to ask Francesca about borrowing things to wear. She'd never get a straight answer from Piano or Carlotta.

She was just clearing away the vast amount of tissue that had been used in the T-shirt packaging when Francesca appeared with an unreadable expression on her face. "Leave that," she said. "I want you at my desk. Come on. Hurry up!"

9

In trouble again

"How on earth did you think this would do?" Francesca was looking more annoyed than Ellie had ever seen her before. "I thought you said you'd read our magazine?"

"Of course I have!"

"Well, if you had you'd know that our readers love Pop 'n' Lolly Lowther. The last thing they want to read is subtle comments that hint at how big-headed Pop is without actually saying it."

"What? I didn't write anything like that!"

Francesca threw a couple of pieces of paper onto her desk. One slid onto the floor and Ellie bent to pick it up. It was a printout of her article, with comments all over it in red pen. "I think you'll find you did," she said coldly. "Trying to live up to your father's reputation by being clever isn't going to take you far. I wanted a simple article about how thrilled you were to meet the Lowthers and instead, amongst the good stuff, you've given me your opinion on why they are splitting up, and all of it, so far as I can see, is totally fabricated." She glared at Ellie. "As if I didn't have enough to do without nurse-maiding a child who thinks she's an investigative reporter!"

Ellie scanned the page hastily. She was almost in tears. "But this isn't what I wrote! I *loved* Pop, *and* Lolly. I did ask why Lolly wanted to become a student, but—"

Francesca wasn't interested in Ellie's protests. "Unfortunately, as we have enough of a crisis on our hands with losing Joe's shoot, we're going to have to use this in some way. If Piano wasn't still working on the pet article

I'd hand it straight to her and send you home, but I can't do that. I don't want Carlotta to handle it either. In spite of what she thinks, editing isn't her strong point."

Francesca was looking through Ellie as she reckoned up her options. Then she focused on her again. "The stupid thing is that the actual writing shows a lot of promise." The way Francesca spoke it didn't exactly sound like a compliment, more a comment made in total frustration, but Ellie felt a small leap of comfort at her words.

Francesca pushed the other sheet of paper in Ellie's direction. "So anyway. I've marked up the article. Go and start putting things right. As soon as Piano has finished she can take over and make sure it's fit to be seen."

A commotion at the front desk made them both turn round. A man with a trolley was backing in through the door. Carlotta was

135

remonstrating with him, but he waved a bit of paper at her.

"You wanted this water!" he shouted before swerving to get past her. "It's your usual order."

"No, we didn't," yelled Piano, joining in. "We cancelled because you never deliver on time."

"Oh for goodness' sake," muttered Francesca. "Do I have to do everything myself?" She left Ellie and strode angrily towards the man with the trolley.

Ellie was aware of the commotion, but she didn't turn to look – she was desperate to see what had gone wrong with her article. How on earth could Francesca have misread it so badly? The answer jumped out at her as soon as she began to read the printout more carefully.

"Someone has altered it!"

The first sentence was in her own words, but as Ellie scanned down the page she could see that a few references to the Lowthers had been changed, so the tone of the article was subtly different from the way she had written it. It was amazing what damage a few changed words could do. Pop was *cold and distant* to her sister, which wasn't true at all. In the article, Ellie had referred with amusement to arguments the twins had told her they'd had while at school, but someone had taken out the added information that, although Pop laughingly admitted she could be argumentative, both girls had told Ellie that they never fell out for long. The bit Ellie had put in about them obviously being very fond of each other, and being totally on each other's wavelength, had vanished.

When it came to Lolly, Ellie almost burst into tears. She had been such a warm, lovely person, and to Ellie it had seemed obvious that she had a real vocation for medicine, but now the article suggested that she was going to university almost to spite her twin sister. Ellie felt like sobbing. She put her head in her hands and stared at the red pen marks scribbled over the words some unknown person had inserted instead of hers. Then she looked up through her fingers at the continuing argument at the door. Francesca was dealing with the situation in her usual efficient way, and Carlotta was taking a call.

It seemed wrong that office life was carrying on while she was so devastated, but she had to pull herself together. The article could be salvaged, and she would be sure to print it out so it couldn't get sabotaged again – and it would be plain to Francesca that Ellie *could* deliver the sort of writing that was wanted. She'd be out of here at the end of the week and whoever had been horrible enough to alter her article wasn't worth worrying about. Even so, she couldn't help wondering who it had been.

Ellie decided that she wouldn't be surprised if it was Piano's idea of a joke. She pretended she was so superior, but Ellie was sure she'd been just as jealous as Carlotta about the interview with the Lowthers. Then another thought struck Ellie. Francesca had said she'd get Piano to tidy the article up once Ellie had done her best with it. Maybe Piano hadn't meant the alterations as a joke at all. Maybe she'd done it so she could write it instead of Ellie! If there was one thing Ellie knew about journalism it was that the more high-profile articles you got published, the better your chances of making a name for yourself. Maybe Piano had decided it would be a waste for a mere student to get her name on the piece, and that she could make better use of the prestige.

That thought made Ellie get on with restoring her article as quickly as she could. She was determined to make it *perfect,* so that Piano wouldn't have the slightest excuse to take it over. She didn't go down to have a cup of tea with Sophie that afternoon. She didn't have time. She needed to stay where she was and get it sorted. As soon as she had finished, she read the piece over one last time and then printed it out. She took it over to Francesca, who was back at her desk again.

Ellie waited anxiously while Francesca quickly read what she had written. "Much better," said Francesca, looking pleased. "When you're not sniping, you can write really well." Ellie was tempted to protest her innocence again, but decided against it. The most important thing was that the Deputy Editor liked her work. Hopefully Angel would too, and the article would appear. It was far more exciting thinking of that, rather than brooding on someone's spitefulness.

Her mum was still out when Ellie got in after work. She made herself a drink and took it up to her bedroom. Hannah was online, so she settled down for a good long chat.

Hi! Good day?

Brilliant! replied Hannah. *More chicks hatched. They're so sweet. How was your day?*

Interesting! wrote Ellie. *Someone ruined my article.*

No way!!!! Tell all.

Ellie's fingers flew over her keyboard. She told Hannah what had happened, who she suspected, and how hard she had worked to get it right again.

Good for you, Hannah wrote approvingly. *Anything else exciting?*

Just some water that turned up after it had been cancelled.

Ha! Your office sounds a shambles! wrote Hannah. *They need you in charge.*

Ellie paused before she replied. She wanted to defend the magazine. The Editorial Department wasn't a shambles. Angel and Francesca set very high standards and they achieved them too. Piano and Carlotta could be

141

spiteful, but that didn't seem to affect their work. The water company messing up was just a nuisance. That sort of thing could happen to anyone. Then she remembered Angel's and Francesca's reactions to Sapphire missing the important fashion shoot. That wasn't just a nuisance. It was a really big deal. They had obviously been shocked as well as angry.

Not a shambles, she wrote, *just bad luck, but it's stressful enough meeting tight deadlines without stuff going wrong.*

Hannah had to go for her dinner, so they signed off and Ellie put her computer to sleep. She sat with her chin in her hands, staring at the blank screen. It probably *was* mostly just bad luck, but it wouldn't hurt to keep her eyes and ears open. After all, her article had been altered deliberately, and she had no proof against Piano. What if, instead of just playing a nasty trick on Ellie, someone was intent on harming the magazine? She'd thought the article had been a personal attack. What if it wasn't, what if it was part of something bigger... like the cancellation of the shoot? Together, those two things had caused a lot more work and had threatened the look of the next issue. Ellie would feel terrible if she didn't act on her instinct. Because that's what it was, instinct; and Ellie Ixos was sure as anything that a good journalist should always be prepared to trust her instinct.

10

Scapegoat

Now Ellie was on the lookout for a troublemaker, she knew she would have to be careful. Instinct was one thing but proof was quite another, and if there really was someone messing things up she would need to be able to prove it; she couldn't accuse anyone without proof. The first thing to do was to write everyone's names down and see who she could eliminate. She got the notebook out of her bag and turned to the page where her father had written *Trust your instincts.*

Ellie stared at the phrase. Okay, but she also needed not to take anyone at face value. Proper detectives had to be capable of seeing what people were *really* like, not how they wanted you to see them.

Ellie took her best pen and thought for a moment. Then she wrote a list of the people she knew who worked for *Heart*.

Angel, Francesca, Piano, Carlotta, Flynn, Sophie, Joe, Uncle Patrick. Of course, lots of other people worked for the magazine in different departments, but she only knew people in editorial, the post room and Flynn who – as one of the IT people – worked in all the departments. She made a note to ask Sophie if anything was going wrong in other offices. She or Flynn would know. Then Ellie remembered that even they were suspects and asking that sort of question might alert them. It wasn't proving very easy, being a detective.

After staring at the list and not having the proof to clear anyone of at least a tiny bit of suspicion, she decided to bide her time and not let her imagination run away with her.

Two things going wrong, however annoying, didn't necessarily make a conspiracy against the magazine. She only had another four days left working there, and her concern would almost certainly come to nothing. Besides, she couldn't think why anyone would make trouble. She wasn't living in a detective story. Things didn't happen like that in real life.

In the morning, Ellie arrived a bit late. Heavy traffic had held her bus up, so it wasn't her fault, but she fully expected someone to tell her off. However, that was the last thing on anyone's mind. Piano and Francesca were crouched in front of the water cooler, and Ellie could see a large patch of wet carpet. What on earth had happened?

"Ellie!" called Francesca, as soon as she noticed her. "Run and fetch more paper towels from the loo. Hurry!"

She took the towels Ellie brought and used

them to soak up a little more water. "Here," she said, standing up and straightening her skirt. "You and Piano carry on. Angel will be here in a minute and I need to get ready. Just do what you can."

"What happened?" asked Ellie, wadding up the towels as best she could, though the paper quickly became soggy and useless.

"Some idiot jammed a load of cups in the cooler so all the water leaked out," said Piano. "You, no doubt."

"Of course I didn't!" protested Ellie.

"Well, since you've been here, all sorts of things have gone wrong," said Piano, getting up. "And as far as I can see, that makes it your fault." She stormed off to her desk, and Ellie watched her go.

How dare Piano blame me, Ellie thought furiously. Then a chill ran through her body. Most of the things that had gone wrong *could* be blamed on a useless person, rather than a

147

vindictive one. If Piano chose to blame her, might the others do the same? Ellie couldn't prove that she hadn't jammed cups under the water cooler, and from Piano's remarks it was obvious that soon everyone would be looking for someone to blame for all their recent misfortune. If Ellie didn't want to be made into a scapegoat she needed to find out who really *was* to blame...and quickly.

And then things got a whole lot worse. A scream of anguish came from the direction of Piano's desk and Francesca, Carlotta and Ellie all stared. Piano had her hands up to her mouth and was staring at the computer screen. "My article! It's all gone Wingdings!"

Francesca got up and went over to Piano. "Whatever do you mean?"

Piano didn't reply. She just pointed one trembling finger at the screen.

Francesca looked. For a moment she paled, then she looked cross. "For goodness' sake,

Piano. You've pressed a wrong button or something. Change it back to your usual font." Francesca went back to her desk and picked up a few sheets of paper. "Ellie, take these into Angel's office and put them on her desk, please. And make sure the cushions on her sofa are properly plumped up. She hates it when they look untidy." She looked thoughtfully at the still-sodden carpet. "I'll put a chair in front of the cooler until the carpet dries out, so no one stands on it."

As Ellie took the papers, Francesca gave her a piercing look. Ellie tried to look as innocent as she felt. Who on earth would have flooded the carpet? And how could she prove that it hadn't been her?

In Angel's office, Ellie was just about to put the papers on the Editor's desk when she noticed a few specks of black dust. Ellie brushed the specks away with her hand. To her horror, instead of disappearing, the specks smeared over the blonde wood of the desk, leaving nasty, black marks. Hastily, Ellie reached into her pocket for a tissue and tried to wipe the desk. But there were more of the tiny black specks everywhere, and the more Ellie rubbed, the worse they got. Ellie tried not to panic, but it wasn't easy. The last thing she wanted was to be caught in Angel's office, smearing black marks over her pristine desk!

Then she remembered the cushions. Francesca had reminded her to plump them up. She went over to the sofa, but realized that her hands were covered in black marks. There was no way she could touch the powder blue cushions with hands like that! And with her heart in her mouth she noticed something else. On the white leather of the sofa were more black specks and there were more still on the white carpet. Surely this wasn't meant as a joke? As Ellie heard Angel approaching she looked at her blackened hands and was sure that she was going to be accused, tried and judged without any means to defend herself.

11
A helping hand

Angel paused at the entrance to her office and glared disapprovingly at Ellie. "What are you doing skulking in my office?"

Ellie tried to hide her dirty hands behind her back. "Um...Francesca asked me to put some things on your desk and to look at your cushions but—"

"But you couldn't simply do it and clear out, you had to poke about in case you found something interesting to report to your uncle."

"No!"

"Get out then. I'll see to the cushions myself."

"But there's..."

Angel plonked Ferdinand in his basket and took off her pale yellow coat. She made to throw it onto the sofa but Ellie yelled just in time.

"Don't!"

Angel stared at her. "Excuse me?"

"Don't put your coat on the sofa. It's all dir—"

But just then another piercing, Piano-voiced scream came from the outer office. Both Angel and Ellie froze and then Angel threw her coat at Ellie. "Hang it up. And then get back to your desk and don't move until someone tells you to. Now!"

Angel watched as Ellie hung the coat up as carefully as she could without smearing it with the black from her hands. She stood to one side to let Ellie out of the office, then she followed Ellie to find out what all the fuss was about.

Francesca was on the phone and Piano had her face in her hands. Carlotta was nowhere to be seen.

"What is all this noise about?" demanded Angel.

Francesca put the phone down and faced the Editor. "Something has gone wrong with the formatting of the magazine articles. I thought it was just a simple mistake when Piano first showed me, but it looks as if it's worse than that. Every article has changed. And when I tried to change the font back from Wingdings to our usual ones, the format was still all wrong. I've just called IT for help."

Angel had a face like thunder, but she spoke calmly, totally in control. "So the content is all right. It's just the formatting that needs redoing?"

Francesca nodded. "So far as I can tell. It's going to take time, but seems to be retrievable. I'd like IT to see if they can find any other nasty surprises though."

"Good thinking." Angel's sharp gaze raked the outer office, like a captain might view his

154

ship in a storm, taking everything in. Her eyes widened slightly when she noticed the chair in front of the water cooler. "Piano, stop being hysterical and put that chair back where it belongs. It looks untidy."

Francesca hardly flinched. "I put it there."

Angel narrowed her eyes. "I assume there was some sort of reason why you wanted to make it difficult for my staff to get a drink of water?"

Ellie found herself feeling sorry for Francesca, but the Deputy Editor was made of stern stuff. "There's been a leak," she said briskly. "The carpet is wet and I didn't want it stepped on until it dries."

Angel frowned. "If anything else goes wrong in this office I shall consider that someone is trying to seriously disrupt the production of our magazine and take steps to get rid of them immediately."

Ellie wanted to voice her agreement, but Angel turned her gaze in Ellie's direction, and she found herself shrinking back against the wall instead. She didn't utter a word until Angel had disappeared into her office. Then she knew she simply *had* to speak. "Francesca!"

"What now?"

"Angel's office. When I went in there was a load of black specks everywhere." She opened her hands. "I tried to clean them off the desk but they smeared. I...I don't know what it is but I managed to stop her throwing her coat on the sofa... *Someone* has got it in for this office. Obviously *I* know it's not me, but I don't know who it is..."

Francesca had stopped listening. "Make yourself scarce, Ellie. I can do without your 'help'." Without another word she hurried towards the Editor's office with an extremely worried expression on her face.

Piano was sitting at her desk looking shocked, while Carlotta was still absent from hers. If Francesca didn't want her, there was only one place that Ellie wanted to be. She headed out of the office and made for the lift.

Fortunately there was no one in the lift, and Ellie had a chance to collect her thoughts. She didn't care any more about being a detective and eliminating all suspects. She was going to trust her instincts on this one. She needed a friend to talk to, and that friend was Sophie. No way could *she* have caused all the havoc in the editorial office. She was as innocent as Ellie herself.

On the basement floor Ellie left the lift and headed to the post room. Sophie would know what to do.

12
Sorting things out

In the post room, Sophie greeted Ellie with her usual grin, but it soon faded when she saw the expression on Ellie's face.

"Whatever's the matter?"

Ellie skirted round a huge cardboard box that had been delivered from a famous fashion designer and dodged behind Sophie's desk. She slumped down at the table and pushed aside a pile of post that Sophie had been sorting.

"I thought I was coming to a brilliant place to do my work experience, but it's a madhouse!"

Sophie grabbed the biscuits and put them in

front of Ellie. Ellie took one and bit into it, speaking through the crumbs. "I tried really hard to be objective, but it's impossible to discover what's going on. I'm sure you and Flynn aren't responsible, but I can't work out who is! I thought it was Piano for a while, but she's gone all hysterical, and then I began to wonder if Francesca had some sort of vendetta going on because of not getting Angel's job like you said, but she's been quite nice to me."

"Whoa there, Ellie." Sophie switched the kettle on and rescued the post from Ellie. She finished sorting it quickly and sat down opposite her. "Where's your evidence? I think you'd better start from the beginning, and if you're thinking of accusing me or Flynn of something you'd better stop eating my biscuits." Sophie sounded annoyed.

"Sorry." Ellie pushed the packet away.

"It's all right. I can see you're in a state." Sophie pushed the packet back after taking one herself. "Start at the beginning and tell me everything."

Ellie did, from her altered article to the problems with the water delivery, the missed photo shoot and then today's dramatic events. "Look at my hands!" said Ellie, putting her biscuit down and showing Sophie her blackened fingers. "I've been set up. How can I prove I didn't mess up Angel's office looking like this?"

"You told me Francesca sent you into Angel's office," Sophie said.

Ellie looked stricken. "Yes. Which *might* mean she's setting me up, but I can't believe it!"

"I think you need to go and wash your hands and calm down," said Sophie. "Go on. I'll still be here when you get back."

Ellie did as Sophie suggested, and she did feel a bit better after scrubbing the black marks off her hands. But as she rejoined Sophie, another thought hit her. "Francesca said she didn't need my 'help'," she told Sophie, "when I was trying to suggest that someone had it in for the magazine." She looked at Sophie, feeling stricken. "I don't *want* it to be Francesca, but I'm getting very afraid that it might be."

Sophie sighed. "You have to be totally certain of your facts before you accuse anyone." She pondered for a minute and then reached for her mobile. "I'm going to text Flynn. This needs more than two brains to work it out."

"It's no good," said Ellie gloomily. "He's going to be up there for ages sorting out the IT problems for them."

"Well until he comes we'll just have to do the best we can without him," said Sophie.

But it wasn't too long before Flynn arrived. The problems hadn't been too difficult to sort out. "Someone had changed all the fonts the magazine uses to Wingdings: you know," said Flynn, "that font with all the meaningless squiggles. Piano had panicked, pressed a few wrong buttons and then panicked even more, but I soon got it sorted out for them. The formatting was all right really. Sometimes it can go a bit weird for no apparent reason. That and the Wingdings thing had them really spooked, but it's okay now."

Sophie opened a new packet of biscuits. "I'll buy the next lot," said Ellie.

"So…" Flynn took the mug of coffee Sophie offered him and sat down. "What's your problem, Ellie?"

"*I* know I didn't do any of this stuff," Ellie said, after explaining everything. "But it all started happening since I arrived, and I'm sure they all think it's my fault." She sighed. "I suppose it doesn't matter in one way because I'll be out of here in a few days, but Uncle Patrick will think I'm useless, and I don't want him to think that. He's just started to take an interest in me and Mum again, and he's the only family we've got."

Flynn frowned. "Well, I can't believe you'll be accused of everything, Ellie, but let's go back to the first time something went wrong. Tell me in as much detail as you can remember what happened the day the shoot was cancelled."

Ellie recounted the day as far as she could remember, up until the point when Francesca had asked her to find the number for the water company so she could cancel the order. Suddenly, Flynn stopped her. "Was that the first time you'd used the database to find a number?" he asked.

Ellie frowned. "Yes, but it's not difficult, Flynn. I'm not stupid."

Flynn smiled at her sympathetically. "Of course you're not. I'm just looking at the problem from as many angles as I can. So you entered the phone number of the water company for Francesca, and handed her the phone. What if you *did* get the wrong number by mistake?"

"Hang on," said Sophie. "If Francesca had got through to the wrong number she'd have known, wouldn't she, as soon as she heard the other person on the line? I mean, most people say the name of the company, don't they?"

"Yes," said Ellie, considering, and trying to be fair. "But the office was manic. While she was dealing with Piano, and making the call, Carlotta butted in with an urgent message, and Francesca was trying to write an article too. I mean, she was seriously distracted."

For a moment they were all silent, then Flynn spoke. "So if Francesca was distracted by the commotion, doesn't that mean that you might have been too, and keyed the wrong number into the phone?"

"No way! Stop thinking it was me!" Ellie was certain. "Look, if I had a computer here I'd show you how I found the number on the database. I can even remember some of it. I think it had several sixes and twos in it.

Numbers stick in my head really easily."

Flynn bent down and picked up his laptop case. "I can get into the database from here," he said, opening it up. "Let's check it out."

In no time he had the database up, and Ellie was searching for the number of the water company in the contacts section. "There!" She stabbed her finger at the screen. They all looked. *Coolwater Company.* There were indeed several sixes and twos in the number.

Flynn scratched his head. "That seems pretty clear." He pulled his phone out of his pocket. "Let's call it." He keyed the number in and waited while it rang. When the call was answered his eyes widened.

"What is it?" hissed Sophie but he ignored her.

Ellie so wished she could hear what was being said.

Flynn cleared his throat. "Sorry," he said into his phone. "What company did you say I'd got through to?" He listened again. "Coolblue Model Agency? I'm so sorry. I seem to have the wrong number." He folded his phone and stared at the girls. "Did you hear that?"

Ellie had her hand to her mouth. "I'm sure that's Sapphire's agency. You know, the model whose appointment was accidentally cancelled. This is awful. It *was* my mistake! Francesca must have cancelled the model instead of the water!"

"Well it's not your fault," said Sophie. "It's Francesca's for allowing herself to be so distracted that she didn't check who she was speaking to – and we can blame the person who messed up inputting those numbers into the database too. Or maybe the file has become corrupted in some way."

"Or maybe *someone* has corrupted it," added Flynn, his fingers flying over the keys of his laptop. "No one could predict that messing up a few numbers in the database would lead to an important assignment being cancelled, that was just tremendous bad luck for *Heart,* but it's the same sort of spitefulness as changing fonts and messing up your article, Ellie. I reckon that all this IT meddling has been done by the same person, and I know how to find out who it was!"

"I knew it was a good idea to get you involved," said Sophie.

"You made up your own password to get into the computer system when you started here, didn't you?" asked Flynn.

Ellie nodded. "I did it with you."

"Of course. And you kept it secret?"

Ellie nodded again.

"Good. Everyone has their own password, which is secret, and as you log on, the system matches your username and the password. If they are correct it lets you in."

"We know this!" said Sophie impatiently.

"But what you might not know," said Flynn,

"is that once you're in, the computer logs every change you make in a transaction history, with the date and your name against it."

"What if you use someone else's computer?" asked Sophie.

"I was told to log out if I have to leave my desk," said Ellie. "And I've seen the others do that too."

"So even if the culprit used someone else's computer she'd still have to log in, and the system would still know who she was. I know how to find that information but most people wouldn't. What filename did you give your article, Ellie?" said Flynn.

Ellie told him and he keyed the name in on a page Ellie had never seen before. Soon, a long list of data came up on the black screen, with dates and names against each line.

"Look," he said. "Every line of data shows a change that's been made to your article."

"Lots of the changes are mine!" said Ellie.

"But then I wrote it."

"But look here," said Flynn. Suddenly there were loads of changes made on the same date by someone who wasn't Ellie. She peered at the screen, but she couldn't make sense of the data. She didn't know anyone's username except her own.

Flynn let out a low whistle and shook his head. "Well I never," he said.

Ellie's heart began to thump. "What?" she said. "I can't understand it. Do you know who altered my article or not?"

"It's there," said Flynn, pointing to the username Ellie couldn't identify. "Plain to see."

"But I don't know who glamgirl *is*!" wailed Ellie.

Flynn looked abashed. "Sorry," he said. "I don't know passwords, of course, but I do know everyone's username. It's Carlotta."

"Carlotta!" Ellie was upset. "But she was *okay* about the interview," she said. "She was

169

jealous to begin with, but I thought she got over it and was fine. She wanted to know all about it afterwards. I thought it was Piano – she's never liked me."

Sophie was looking serious. "Can you check the other stuff?" she said.

"Of course," said Flynn. "I'll look at the fonts first."

Ellie held her breath as he scrolled through and found the right files. It only took a few minutes to check. The fonts had been changed early that morning.

"Glamgirl," said Sophie in a flat voice.

"But why?" said Ellie. "She's got a job that loads of people would *die* for."

Sophie shrugged and Flynn shook his head. He looked even more serious than he had before. "I ought to check the database now," he said. "Of course lots of people alter bits of the database as information changes, but their usernames will be against every alteration. We

170

can easily find out who last altered the water cooler information." He worked away for a few minutes while the girls waited anxiously. When he found the file it didn't come as a surprise to any of them.

"Carlotta again."

"That's it then," said Sophie. "That's plenty of proof for you, Ellie. No one can possibly blame you for anything now. She must have arrived at the office before anyone else, altered the fonts, and probably flooded the carpet and dropped something black and horrible all over Angel's office as well. No question!"

Flynn was still looking serious. "What's worrying me most though," he said, "is how many other database entries she may have changed. It'll take ages to trawl through all of the transaction history, and meanwhile the magazine probably has dodgy data to work with." He closed the lid of his laptop. "The information will all need checking and putting

171

right. It'll take time and money, and meanwhile, other mistakes could be made. Ellie, I think you and I need to speak to Angel, right away."

13

A culprit accused

On the way up in the lift, Ellie's stomach was churning. She could see that Flynn was right. Every department in the magazine relied on the database for so many things, from contacts to staff details, advertisers and suppliers – all the little bits of information that, put together, helped the whole magazine to run efficiently. It might take ages to correct, and until it was corrected, no one would be able to trust its information. Angel needed to know what had been going on in her department, but all the same, Ellie wasn't looking forward to bringing bad news.

Up in the Editorial Department it was

uncharacteristically quiet. For a few moments Ellie wondered what was wrong. Then she realized that some major changes had been made. Angel was sitting at Francesca's desk with Ferdinand's basket at her feet. Francesca was using Piano's desk and Piano was sharing the reception desk with Carlotta. Piano was even more straight-faced than usual, and Carlotta looked away as they came in.

"I expect Angel has cleared out of her office until it's been cleaned," Ellie whispered to Flynn.

Angel had a collection of fashion photographs on the desk and was sifting through them, accepting some and rejecting the others. When she became aware of Flynn and Ellie approaching she looked up with huge irritation.

"We need to speak to you," said Flynn, seemingly immune to Angel's hostility. "In private."

Angel looked through them both. "Speak to Francesca," she said. "She'll let me know if it's important enough for me to spend any time on."

Ellie felt angry. She'd screwed up her courage to speak to Angel and she wasn't going to let herself be put off. "Francesca ought to know too," she said to Angel. "But we came to you first because you're in charge."

Angel narrowed her eyes. She ignored Ellie and looked at Flynn. "Well?"

"We know who has been messing things up in the department," he said in a low voice. "Amongst other things, they've been putting the wrong information into the database."

"It could be serious for the whole magazine," added Ellie urgently.

Angel looked directly at Ellie for the first time. "I hardly need you to tell me what could be serious," she said.

Ellie blushed.

Angel called to her deputy. "Francesca!"

The Deputy Editor got up and joined them.

"Flynn here has some important information for us," said Angel. "We will go into the boardroom. Ellie, fetch us coffee."

"You'll need Ellie too," Flynn said quickly. "She was the person who alerted me to all this."

Angel raised her eyebrows, but made no objections. Francesca gave the coffee order to Piano and Ellie followed Angel, Francesca and Flynn along the corridor and into the boardroom.

Ellie had never been in the boardroom before. She looked about her with interest. This must be where Uncle Patrick came to have meetings with Angel and the rest of the board members. Important deals were probably done here. In the centre of the room was a large, highly polished table in pale wood, with chairs equally spaced around it. Angel waited for

Flynn to pull out the chair at the top of the table, then she sat down on it. Francesca sat to one side of her and Flynn to the other. After some hesitation, Ellie sat next to Flynn.

"So," said Angel, looking at Ellie. "This had better be good. No childish tale-telling please."

Ellie swallowed. She entwined her hands under the table and tried to gather her thoughts. Then she remembered her father's first words in his notebook. *You can do this.* She cleared her throat and began.

"The cancelling of Sapphire's photo shoot, the font problems and...um...the black specks in your office. They all point to one person."

Angel looked very angry. "You'll need some pretty convincing proof before I take your word against any of my staff," she said.

Flynn rescued Ellie. He pulled out his laptop and showed Angel what he'd found.

"It's still possible that someone else might

have obtained Carlotta's password and username, and be framing her," Angel said thoughtfully.

Flynn nodded. "Possible, yes," he said. "But we have her logging in exceptionally early today, and the keystrokes to prove she changed the fonts. To have caused the flood and made your office dirty someone would have had to come in very early, before anyone else."

"There's a CCTV camera in the main entrance of the building," said Angel. "Francesca, get someone to check the film. It'll show if it was Carlotta who came in before anyone else."

Francesca picked up the phone and rang down to the main reception. "I'll hold," she said into the phone, after explaining what she wanted.

"The black marks were toner, from the printer in my office," said Angel, breaking the silence while Francesca waited for the information they needed. "No doubt there are fingerprints all over the empty cartridge we found in my wastepaper basket."

"What I don't understand…" Ellie began.

Angel turned her steely gaze on Ellie, and Ellie blushed.

"Well, why would she do all these things just because I got the interview? I know she was jealous of me, but why your office…?"

Angel had a wry expression on her face. "This is a tough business," she told Ellie, addressing her kindly for the first time. "You might have noticed."

Ellie nodded.

"It affects different people in different ways," said Angel. "Some make it, but many don't. Some of them leave because they can't take it, others become malicious and hang around to watch the havoc they cause. Carlotta will have had her reasons. Maybe being passed over when Piano became my PA, even though she's only been with us a few months. That's the sort of thing that can make people bitter. I very much doubt it's all to do with you, Ellie. You're not *that* important."

Ellie blushed again.

Francesca put the phone down and everyone looked at her. "Carlotta was one of the earliest people in today," she said. "And the first in this office by some time."

"If Carlotta can learn to channel her feelings more usefully," said Angel in a steely voice, "she'll probably go far. But not in *my* magazine." She looked at her Deputy Editor. "I'll see her now. You'd better send her in."

As soon as Francesca had gone to fetch Carlotta, Angel gave Flynn and Ellie a brief smile. "Thank you for putting the magazine first," she said. "You'd better get back to your jobs."

Flynn opened the door for Ellie, but as they stepped out into the corridor, Carlotta pushed past and flounced into the boardroom, looking flushed and angry.

"It doesn't look as if she's about to go quietly," whispered Flynn.

Carlotta hadn't bothered to close the door behind her, and Ellie and Flynn could hear almost every word she said. Angel's words were more indistinct, but she must have been asking Carlotta if she was responsible for everything that had recently gone wrong.

"This magazine stinks!" spat Carlotta. "You all deserved what you got."

Again, Angel's words were quietly spoken, but Carlotta's reply was shouted.

"I should have got the job!" she yelled. "I'm worth ten of *her*. And that pathetic *student*…"

Flynn took Ellie's arm and guided her away. "I think we've heard enough," he said. "Angel wasn't far wrong. Carlotta does seem to have a huge chip on her shoulder."

Carlotta came back out, slamming the door behind her. She caught sight of Ellie and scowled. "Nasty little *sneak!*" she said, before pushing past.

"Pay no attention," said Flynn.

"I won't," said Ellie, but even so, the venom in Carlotta's voice had upset her. No one liked to be called a sneak. "Do you think anyone would mind if I went down to help Sophie instead of going back into the office just now?" she asked him.

"I'm sure they won't," he said. "Come on, let's go together. The IT Department can spare me for another five minutes."

"Thanks," said Ellie, fighting back the tears that threatened to fall. "This has been a bit more stressful than I'd anticipated."

Down in the basement, Ellie helped Sophie frank some mail. Francesca had rung down at Angel's request, to find out if she was there, and make sure she was all right. It seemed the Editor cared a bit more about her young work placement student than Ellie had thought, which was nice to know.

Ellie was just putting the franked mail in a sack, feeling much calmer, when she heard a voice she thought she recognized, speaking to Sophie.

"I was told I'd find Ellie Ixos here," it said.

Ellie looked up. "That's me," she said with a smile. "And I think you must be my Uncle Patrick."

The man smiled. "Well deduced," he said, offering his hand for her to shake. "I've spoken to you on the phone a few times. But I haven't seen you in years. Goodness, you've grown up to look like your dad!"

"*You* look like my dad too," said Ellie, thinking of a photograph she had.

For a moment they simply looked at each other, and then Uncle Patrick cleared his throat. "I was wondering," he said, "if you were free for lunch?"

14
An invitation

It had been a brilliant day at school. Ellie had the latest copy of *Heart* in her bag, but she hadn't needed to take it out to show anyone. All her friends had bought copies and it seemed they had *all* brought them to school. Even Ellie's English teacher had read and enjoyed the article.

"I am *so* jealous!" squealed Kate. Her copy of the magazine was opened at the double-page article about the Lowther twins.

"You and POP!" shrieked Lizzie.

Ellie put her hands over her ears. "I was *sooo* lucky," she said modestly.

Hannah stabbed her finger at a picture of Ellie standing between the two Lowthers.

"You look so cool. That dress! Where on earth did you get it?"

"It was my gran's."

"Wow."

Now Ellie was walking up the path to her flat, happy at how fortunate she was to have friends who were pleased at her success, not sour and jealous like Carlotta had been. As she opened the door the phone was ringing, so she dropped her bag on the floor and ran to answer it. It was Uncle Patrick.

"Hi!"

"Hi!" said Ellie.

"I like your article. I've got it here. Well done!"

Ellie glowed with pleasure. "Thank you. And thanks again for getting me the work placement. I couldn't have done it without your help."

"Oh, I don't know about that," he said with

a laugh. Then his voice changed. It sounded a bit awkward, even shy. "Ellie?"

"Yes?"

"Is your mum in?"

"No. She doesn't get in from work for another hour."

"Oh."

Ellie couldn't tell if her uncle was pleased or sad.

"Look, would you tell her I called, and say I'd like to speak to her. We need to meet, and talk. It's been a long time…and…well I hope we can be friends. I really do. Will you let her know?"

"Of course I will."

"I'll ring again. I promise."

Ellie put the phone down, and looked at herself in the hall mirror. Her excited face, with her hair all tangled from the windy weather, gazed back at her. She wondered what her dad would have thought of all this. She was sure he'd have been happy to think of his family being back in touch again. She hoped he'd have been pleased with, and proud of, her ambition too. A bit of her felt sad that he wasn't here with her, but she had his notebook, with his wise thoughts inside it to help her on her way.

She took off her coat, and went to hang it up. Then she noticed the post, sticking through the letter box. She pulled it out and took it through to the kitchen. While the kettle boiled she sorted through it. There were two pizza offers and a couple of letters that looked like bills for her mum. There was also, unusually, a letter for her. She turned it over and noticed that it had been franked in the *Heart* post room. Who could be writing to her from the magazine?

She sat down with a mug of coffee and opened the letter. There was the familiar headed paper that she had had such trouble folding on her first day. This page had been folded immaculately, and she wondered, with a giggle, if Piano had been asked to do it. She glanced to the bottom of the letter, and saw to her surprise that it was from Angel.

Dear Ellie, it said. *I am sorry that your time with us was coloured by an unfortunate chain of events. However, I wanted to thank you officially for your role in putting things right, and to assure you that your time with us hasn't gone unnoticed.*

I have decided that I would like to offer you the opportunity to work with us again. We realize that you have school commitments, but would be pleased if you would call into the office during your next holiday. We can't promise to give you all the celebrity interviews, but we can offer you the opportunity to hone your skills until you leave school and decide whether you want to pursue journalism as a career. If you would like to do this, please ring the office and arrange a time to call.

Yours, Angel Makepiece
Editor in Chief

Ellie read the letter. Then she read it again. It was wonderful! She would be able to go back, to see Sophie and Flynn again, and to be a proper journalist – almost. How fantastic!

She couldn't wait to tell Hannah and the rest of her friends, but even more she could hardly wait for the next few weeks to pass, so that she could catch the bus, walk up the road, and go back to work at *Heart, the magazine to die for!*

To find out what happens next behind the scenes at Heart Magazine read

My life behind the scenes at...

Heart Magazine

Celebrity

Pop

Boys, blues & shoes

Gossip

2 Cindy Jefferies

ISBN: 9781409520214

Cindy Jefferies is the author of the fabulous

Fame School

Look out for:

Reach for the Stars
Rising Star
Secret Ambition
Rivals!
Tara's Triumph
Lucky Break
Solo Star
Christmas Stars
Pop Diva
Battle of the Bands
Star Maker
Dancing Star
Summer Spectacular
Trick or Treat

For more stylish reads
check out
www.fiction.usborne.com